Love is
a time of enchantment:
in it all days are fair and all fields
green. Youth is blest by it,
old age made benign:
the eyes of love see
roses blooming in December,
and sunshine through rain. Verily
is the time of true-love
a time of enchantment — and
Oh! how eager is woman
to be bewitched!

DOM

Library at Home Service
Community Services
Hounslow Library, CentreSpace
24 Treaty Centre, High Street
Hounslow TW3 1ES

YOUR COMMUNITY
YOUR SERVICES

0	1	2	3	4	5	6	7	8	9
754	081	532		6464	995	30736	367	818	409
	7751	3002	803		337₈	346	507	818	947 033
		3057J				6306			637
		862	3186	3085			3457		
							7927		
		943		3415					

P10-L-2061

A HOUSE CALLED SANCTUARY

When her property-developer boss sends her to a quiet Devon village, Robin Ford finds herself at the centre of a local conflict — should Sennerton House remain standing or should a new holiday complex rise in its place? Village feelings run high, and Robin's problem is made harder when she finds both leaders of the sparring parties equally attractive! During the times ahead, Robin learns that there is more to life than a London flat and a well-paid job . . .

Books by Christina Green
in the Ulverscroft Large Print Series:

MISTRESS OF MOORHILL
THE SONG OF THE PINES

CHRISTINA GREEN

A HOUSE CALLED SANCTUARY

Complete and Unabridged

ULVERSCROFT
Leicester

First published in Great Britain in 1985 by
Robert Hale Limited
London

First Large Print Edition
published October 1992
by arrangement with
Robert Hale Limited
London

British Library CIP Data

Green, Christina
A house called Sanctuary.—Large print ed.—
Ulverscroft large print series: romance
I. Title
823.914 [F]

ISBN 0–7089–2728–9

Published by
F. A. Thorpe (Publishing) Ltd.
Anstey, Leicestershire
Set by Words & Graphics Ltd.
Anstey, Leicestershire
Printed and bound in Great Britain by
T. J. Press (Padstow) Ltd., Padstow, Cornwall

1

"ROBIN, I want a word with you!"

Derek Harman's voice echoed down the corridor and Robin sighed — why couldn't he behave as other bosses did? Give instructions over his desk, put them on tape, even write her a memo . . . he really was the end.

Irritated, she rose and went to the door of her office, just in time to see him disappearing into his own room, a stocky, middle-aged man in a hurry. By the time she got there he was on his way out again, a brief-case and keys juggled in one hand, the other holding a file which he threw at her.

She caught it neatly, well-practised in this chaotic form of communication. "Where are you off? I thought we were both going down to Devon today to look at that old house?"

His eyes twinkled, as if it was the biggest joke imaginable to leave his personal assistant, unbriefed and completely unprepared, to cope with the pre-purchase survey of a potentially valuable property.

"Sorry, love, but trouble's blown up in the new development in the Midland — I've got to rush. You'll have to go to Devon on your own."

"Oh, Derek, really! But I don't know a thing about it — ." Robin's voice was sharp. Derek merely grinned and proceeded on his way, his voice flying back over his shoulder and finally fading as he went through the lift door. "Not to worry, all the guff's in the file. You'll soon see what's what. Oh — don't forget — the new owner of the place, Guy, somebody-or-other, is due to ring at any moment. Use that well-known efficiency and charm of yours, soothe him down, tell him it's all under control, that you'll report back to me about the state of the property and I'll be in touch with him later. Don't know why he's in such a rush to sell; the place appears to have been derelict for years. Well, I'm off. Cheers . . . "

And *clang* went the lift door, with

a sound of doom.

Robin turned on her heel, passing the room where the three typists clattered noisily at their machines, and returned to her own office, colour high and temper rising to match. What a nerve the man had got! She'd taken it for five years, ever since she joined Harman Developments Ltd. as an inexperienced but ambitious secretary, but now she had reached the heady position of Personal Assistant to the Managing Director, why should she accept such cavalier treatment any longer? One of these days she'd walk out on him . . .

All these thoughts were familiar ones and, as usual, in a short time Robin was smiling again. She loved her job, enjoyed the work, and, apart from his mercurial comings and goings, knew that Derek wasn't a bad boss.

So she sat down, grabbed the file he'd flung at her and tried hard to concentrate on the matter in hand. As Derek had said, this Guy somebody-or-other would be ringing soon and she was determined to uphold her reputation of coolly efficient, practical, unemotional and first-class personal assistant.

When the phone rang she had all the information at her finger-tips and felt smugly confident. The caller's voice was deep and attractive.

"Mr Harman, please. It's Guy Devenish."

"I'm sorry, Mr Devenish, but Mr Harman's away for a few days. He asked me to take your call. I'm Robin Ford, his personal assistant. May I help you?"

"Well — " He sounded put off; probably one of those chauvinistic males, she decided promptly, who didn't think a mere woman could do a man's job. That made her tighten her lips and say, firmly but pleasantly, "I've got the file on Sentry House in front of me. I'm going down there myself very shortly to look at the property."

"I see . . . "

She grinned; he sounded impressed now.

"Well, Miss Ford, in that case obviously you know what I'm talking about."

They talked on for five minutes and at the end of that time her shrewd questioning and quick grasp of his replies

4

allowed her to take hold of the situation, and resulted in his tone becoming even more agreeable.

"It all sounds very organised at your end, Miss Ford. I hope Mr Harman will decide to go ahead and buy, once the survey is done — the old place is a mere shell now, and it seems sensible to sell it for redevelopment. His idea is to rebuild, I believe?"

She flipped through the file rapidly. "Yes, a holiday complex. The southwest area is a very popular holiday area now, and the complex he has in mind would be highly commercial — chalets as well as a camping ground, lodges in the woods, a swimming pool, pitch and putt course, children's playground — you know the sort of thing, I'm sure."

"Sounds a great idea." He laughed, a warm, deep sound, and then added thoughtfully, "But I can't help wondering what the village will make of it!"

Robin's eyebrows shot up. "Surely there couldn't be any objections? Nobody wants an old house hanging about these days. And the holiday complex would provide local employment, more trade in the village, why, it would do nothing but good!"

"You've got a point there, Miss Ford. But all the same — Sennerton is a tiny, remote place and I can't see its inhabitants welcoming quite such drastic changes. However, progress can't be stopped, eh? Well, many thanks for your help. I shall be looking forward to hearing from Mr Harman when you've reported back to him. I hope to return to South Africa, where my business is based, within the next fortnight, if possible; so I'd like to think things could be settled by then — "

"If there are no hitches, Mr Devenish, the sale can go straight through."

"Excellent. Well, thanks again, Miss Ford. And goodbye."

"Goodbye to you, Mr Devenish."

She thought he'd sounded attractive and pleasant; quite a devastating combination. She wondered idly if they were likely to meet within the course of the next two weeks; it was a pleasing thought.

★ ★ ★

EXETER, proclaimed the motorway sign, and Robin braked slowly and steadily. The white Mini slid back into the slow lane, eventually turning off the busy conveyor-belt of incessant traffic, heading for the distant city with its sun-touched twin spires and looping boundary of gleaming river.

She sighed impatiently. Another few miles and she would be at Sennerton, the village containing old Sentry House. The irritation she had felt earlier this morning at Derek's sudden departure returned once more.

As she drove off the motorway into quieter country roads, the remoteness and strangeness of the surrounding landscape intensified her annoyance. After London's friendly rush and bustle, she didn't feel at all at home here among these high-hedged lanes and tall, skeletal winter trees. And it was such a lonely landscape — billowing bare hills with only occasional clusters of buildings, which she guessed were farms, dotted about like small grey mushrooms, overshadowed by the winter tracery of woodland and hedgerow.

If only Derek had come down with her

the job could be finished far sooner than she could possibly do it on her own; she was bound to stay for, at least, a couple of days. A good thing there was a pub in the village with accommodation. She had rung the Black Dog before she left town; the landlord, country-voiced and slow of speech, had sounded a real rustic. What on earth was she letting herself in for? Lumpy beds, home cooking and lukewarm bath water . . .

At this point, she came to a four crossway with no sign to guide her. Irritation arose, even stronger. Which lane led to Sennerton for goodness' sake? Straight ahead looked narrower and bushier than ever; she chose the left hand lane hopefully, and drove on.

Suddenly a tractor came hurtling around a corner, and she trod on the brake pedal with her heart beating rapidly. Some drivers shouldn't be allowed on the road! Angrily she waited for the man to back, but no, he was making obvious signs that she should do so. Unwinding the window, she stuck her head out.

"Surely you can back up?" she said, annoyed.

"Sorry — quicker if you do." The man had a country voice and was shabbily dressed.

Tight-lipped, she reversed the Mini down the twisting lane to the four crossway and the tractor rattled past, the driver giving her a grin and a wave.

Once again, she set off only to find that her chosen route ended in the entrance to a newly ploughed field. Robin's annoyance mounted. Back to the unmarked cross roads and try again. Unfairly, and with considerable heat, she began wishing that Derek was here, sharing this hassle with her. Well, she would make sure he heard about it when she got back to London!

This time the unlikely lane proved to be the right choice for, suddenly and unexpectedly, she came around a sharp corner and had to brake fast, for there was the sign, half-hidden under the over-hanging hedge —

SENNERTON
PLEASE DRIVE SLOWLY
THROUGH THE VILLAGE

Robin heaved a sigh of frustration. She had nearly run into the back of a herd of slow-moving brown cows. Just in front of her, a battered Landrover inched along, encouraging the animals to keep moving, while an energetic black and white dog yapped frantically as it herded them through the narrow street, finally following them into a muddy farm yard.

Cottage doors were closed and curtains drawn, Robin saw. It was like a village of the dead — but no, suddenly a woman came down the road, peering into the car with undisguised curiosity. Uncertain whether to be angry or amused, Robin parked the Mini beside a tall, greystone wall not far from the inn where she had booked her room.

The ancient sign over the Black Dog swung and creaked unmusically as the winter wind slapped at it. Robin longed for a comforting cup of tea, but decided it was more important to look at Sentry House while it was still light.

She left the car, heading instinctively towards the church, set on a slope a hundred yards up the road. Where was the old house? The village was so small, surely it couldn't be far away — round a corner, suddenly, she came upon it; Sentry House, tall, gaunt and obviously derelict, standing at the end of a long drive framed by over-grown bushes and tall, bare-branched trees.

Robin stopped in mid-step and stared. What a mouldering pile, neglected and quite useless . . . no wonder Guy Devenish wanted to be rid of it. Her long-standing irritation at having been sent to Sennerton on her own began to fade. Here was the sort of job she enjoyed doing, and at once she felt she wanted to get on and do it. Briskly, she went up the drive, feet crunching noisily on the weed-scattered gravel.

The house drew nearer, its black hulk sending heavy shadows over the surrounding wild grounds. As Robin stepped into the shadow she felt a chillness descend upon her; the frail winter sunshine had been left behind and she had to refocus her eyes to peer up at the house through the semi-darkness.

She made a few notes, rapidly and efficiently. Lintels and frameworks were rotting, stonework bulging ominously. The crumbling front steps were negotiable after a fashion, so cautiously she climbed into the lofty hallway. Rafters were poised perilously with few supports; it wouldn't take more than a good hefty push to send them tumbling, she guessed.

Something flapped past her, brushing her head as it went, and a gust of wind moaned eerily down the shattered staircase. Robin told herself sternly not to be foolish — but her pulses beat a tattoo, and she was more than ready to leave Sentry House to its decaying memories. It was ridiculous of her to be afraid — after all, she'd had five years of inspecting old houses — but there did seem to be a peculiar sort of atmosphere here. A feeling . . .

Suddenly there was an unmistakable footstep on the gravel path outside and, once again, her pulses raced.

"Who's there? Who is it?" She heard her voice grow shrill and edgy and, in a burst of annoyance at her alarm, reminded herself that it was probably pure imagination that had made her think she heard someone approaching.

But a hunched figure slowly loomed out of the shadows, and she saw brilliant eyes staring at her from an ancient, beaky face. She couldn't stop the little choking cry that came, unbidden, to her lips. Memories of horror stories raced through her churning mind, and so it was with immense relief that she heard a mild voice say, "Sorry I scared 'ee, m'dear — jest looking at me cabbages, I was, and I heard 'ee moving round inside and thought mebbe I'd better have a look-see . . . dunno who were most scared, you or me!"

Once the initial terror of his sudden appearance had worn off Robin saw the bulky figure was an old man dressed in even older clothes, his long, weather-beaten face crowned by an antiquated and battered tweed hat. The oldest inhabitant, of course, or Worzel Gummidge himself . . .

Quite recovered from her fright, she smiled and went down the uneven steps until she stood beside him. "I'm sorry, too," she said cheerily, "I was just having a wander around."

"Oh ah." The old man looked a bit

of a country yokel, but his grey eyes were astute. "Visiting the village, are you, then?"

"That's right." Abruptly, Robin remembered Guy Devenish's words ... *I wonder what the village will make of it* ... Surely this was a heaven sent opportunity to find out? She bit back the words proclaiming her name and mission, and carefully prompted the old man to talk, instead.

"Sennerton's a quaint little place — you live here, of course?"

"Man an' boy. Nigh on seventy year, come the spring."

"That's a long time. You must have seen a few changes along the way — "

"Oh ah. This house now — lived in by old Sir Bart when I were a boy, it were. Cared for proper, full o' staff gardens all kept up. Terrible the way it's gone now." He heaved a sigh and stared up at the crumbling facade.

"It's certainly a mess. Beyond hope, I'd say." Robin looked at the old man expectantly. The shadows were darkening and it was increasingly difficult to see his face clearly. But at her last words a gleam

14

came into his hooded eyes and he said sharply, "Never! Not Sentry! Why, there's still plenty of hope left in the old house yet! With a history like what it's got, it'd be a sin to say no hope . . . " He turned back, peering up at the overhanging bulk of crumbling masonry and tiny, broken leaded window panes, mumbling to himself, and Robin felt herself stirred by some strange, unfamiliar reaction.

"What do you mean, history? Did something special happen here, then? I thought it was just a Victorian mansion, built on an older site — " She tailed off craftily. If she wanted more information — and of course she did — it wouldn't do to let the old boy know that she had prior knowledge of the house.

She recalled that the file Derek had thrown at her this morning had contained lists of Sentry House deeds that dated far back into the past. The deeds themselves were held by Guy Devenish's solicitors, but the schedule in the file had started with a fourteenth century date. Up there in a modern office block in central London, the fact hadn't seemed important, but here at Sennerton, beside the ruins of the old house itself, with the atmosphere of past years running riot around her, it had become very important indeed.

She went across to the old man, now a mere shape in the encroaching darkness, and put a hand on his arm. "Please tell me about it — about the history of the house, Mr — er — Mr . . . ."

She caught a flash of white teeth as he turned. Keen eyes gleamed approvingly at her. "Bert Woodall, m'dear, call me Bert, everyone do."

"Thank you, Bert, I'd like to. And — ." Something instinctive and cautious stopped her completing the sentence by adding her own name. Luckily, he didn't ask, but started at once to tell her about the house, his obvious enthusiasm colouring his lazy, country voice. "A priory it were, oh, a long time ago — hundreds of years, so they do say. And that's when the Rights started, see."

"The — Rights?"

"Rights o' Sanctuary. How it got its name, see? Sanctuary — Sentry — same word. *And* the village, too; well, Sennerton's not so different from

16

Sentry, now, is it?"

"No. I hadn't thought — how interesting. Do go on, Bert."

"Well, these 'ere Rights meant that anyone wanting help, or needing to escape from a bit o' trouble, could go to the priory and be taken in, see, fer forty days. Safe, they were, in Sentry. No one could get at them there."

"I see. And after the forty days were up?"

"Well, seems then they had to make up their minds — either leave the country, fer good, or give 'emselves up and take what's coming."

"Fascinating!" Robin was held in a little spell of surprise and unexpected appreciation. Abruptly she realised how little we know of other people's lives — whether of today or yesterday.

Beside her, Bert shuffled restlessly, his bright eyes cocked up at the first stars that winked faintly in the dark vault above them.

"Here, I've been chatting on fer too long! Must get back to my tea. You coming, Miss? I'll show 'ee my cabbages as we go."

Together they walked back down the long gravelled drive, Bert droning on about the wet winter and the poor vegetable crop. Robin said nothing except, occasionally — "I see" and "really?" — but her mind was, nevertheless, fully occupied.

It was as if the village had cast a spell upon her. All the irritation she had felt earlier in the day had gone, she even smiled broadly as she remembered Derek flitting in and out of her office, shouting ineffectual instructions at her. Now she was actually here in Sennerton she felt quite differently about the project he had so craftily thrown into her lap. Why, she might even enjoy her few days here! If all the villagers were as friendly and helpful as Bert was, then her task would be quick and easy.

As Bert paused to bend over the iron railings at the end of the drive, pointing at a few rows of soggy cabbages, Robin glanced back and, as the moon slid out from behind racing clouds, beaming down a strong, enchanted light, saw Sentry House standing there, black and imposing, its ugly deterioration hidden in shadow, its elegant, rambling outline an unforgettable sight against the dramatic backdrop of wintry sky.

A new, strange emotion touched her, an unexpected feeling, one she'd never experienced before. It was as if she belonged here in Sennerton, here at Sentry House —

Bert tugged at her arm. "You staying at the Black Dog? Turn left by the church and you can't miss it. Well, g'night, then, Miss." He lifted a horny forefinger to the brim of his ancient hat, and went off up the road.

* * *

There were welcoming lights shining through the windows of the Black Dog, and Robin went in with glad expectancy. All that standing about in the cold with old Bert had made her long for a cup of tea and a cosy warm-up by a country fire.

The landlord took her bag and led her up creaky, twisting stairs with a friendly smile. She soon learned that he had a ready tongue.

19

"Had a good journey down from London, then, Miss Ford? You'll find it a bit different down here, I daresay — quieter, too — the only noises we get are Farmer Wells' darned cockerel first thing in the morning and old Chatterbox up along in Sentry grounds."

She was shown into a charming little room with a chintz-curtained window which overlooked the road. She smiled as she looked around, feeling at home already. "Yes, London does seem a long way off. Who's old Chatterbox, by the way?"

As if in answer, an agonised shriek came echoing through the peaceful village and Robin blanched thinking some poor soul was being attacked.

"That's him now — the donkey belonging to the gypsies. You'll get used to him if you stay long enough!" The man put her bag on an old-fashioned cane chair by the window and then paused as he went out of the room. "You'd like some tea, I expect? I'll get my wife to bring some up. And though we don't do evening meals, there'll be snacks in the bar from seven o clock . . . anything you need, Miss Ford, please ask — we're here to make you, comfortable, remember."

"Thank you, Mr — ?"

"Ted Mullins, Miss Ford. Call me Ted."

She returned his smile as his closed the door behind him, and began unpacking her bag, reflecting on the warmth of her welcome here in Sennerton. Funny how things turned out — rarely as you expected them to.

2

LATER, having had her tea and spent a busy couple of hours beginning her report on Sentry House, Robin felt she could now relax and sample the hospitality that was being offered in the bar.

She went down the dark stairs and found her way into a long, narrow taproom, where a huge logfire blazed at one end, and candles stuck in bottles gave a dim, cosy light. With a drink on the table at her side, she settled comfortably in the far corner, feeling the welcome heat of the fire permeate her whole body, relaxing her, until she was as contented as a purring cat, basking in a favourite seat.

Ted Mullins, she decided approvingly, was a proper landlord, with a friendly word for all his customers. He came across from the bar to throw another log on the fire, asking attentively, "Anything you want, Miss Ford? How about a nice bowl of game soup, and a beef curry to follow? I can recommend them both — just had 'em for my own tea . . . "

"Sounds great, Mr Mullins — sorry, Ted! I didn't realise I was so hungry." As she waited for the food, Robin took a good look at the other people in the bar. Only a handful at the moment, but it was early and doubtless the place would fill up as the evening progressed.

One or two customers were leaning against the long bar, talking quietly, their conversations rising and falling like the gentle hum of bees, the country voices weaving a rustic charm. They talked quietly about the weather, next market day, the price of beef . . . Robin's eyelids drooped sleepily.

Then she jumped as the door banged open and two men entered, stamping heavy boots, ordering their beer and talking together in loud, uncaring voices. Abruptly, Robin was wide awake and interested, unashamedly eavesdropping.

"You're a fool not to see it my way, Nip. Of course, If Sentry goes, then we go too, but till then, I'm fer staying. I'm getting too soft to go on the road again, and the old 'van's not exactly roadworthy either . . . no, no, we'd all best stay put and see what happens. Mebbe the old place'll jest be built up again."

Something about the man's features impressed themselves on Robin's busily conjecturing mind. The swarthy complexion, the heavy nose — could he be a gypsy? Ted Mullins had mentioned that the donkey belonged to a gypsy. She listened intently, as the other man had his say.

"No, Charlie, that's a lot o'nonsense. Now's the time to go, before all the trouble starts. I told 'ee I'd heard that someone's coming down to look at the house — well, for sure that means things'll be happening soon. If we leave in a day or so we can camp further down the valley, where the spring flowers are. Dorrie knows all about them wild daffies, been picking them since a child, 'er has. And they'll fetch a pretty penny, come Easter."

Charlie swigged his beer in a gargantuan gulp and growled back, "Nah! I'm stayin', me and Britt and the young 'un, we don't move on till we have to. You go if you must, but you'm a fool to do so — "

Robin watched a deep frown convert Nip's rugged face into black anger, and felt uneasiness grow inside her. There was a suppressed conflict between the two men that travelled the length of the bar.

Just as she was wondering what might happen next, again the door opened and another man entered. She looked at him critically — something vaguely familiar about him, wasn't there? Youngish, not bad looking, with bright blue eyes and sandy hair. A farmer, obviously, for he wore muddy Wellingtons and had an unmended tear in his shabby tweed jacket. Suddenly she remembered — he was the tractor driver who had made her back down the lane at the four crossway. She didn't expect him to notice her in the corner by the fire, and so the astute, brief stare that came her way was quite a surprise.

Ted reached for a tankard and smiled at the newcomer. "Evening, Tom. Usual?"

"Please."

Robin listened edgily for his next words, noting the slight country burr and thinking it really rather charming.

"I've brought in a copy of the poster for you, Ted — put it up somewhere, will you?"

The landlord pushed a pint of beer across the counter and took the proffered roll of paper. "I certainly will. The more people who see this the better, eh, Tom? Think you'll get a good turn-out?"

Robin hardly heard Tom's reply, for all her attention was suddenly riveted upon the poster which Ted was tacking to the wall beside the bar. It was headed — KEEP SANCTUARY OPEN. Her interest flared and she read on, suddenly realising that there were unexpected issues involved with Sentry House — just as Guy Devenish had hinted.

The poster was well-produced, suggesting financial means and strong support; it announced a meeting to be held shortly at Well Farm in the village, inviting all those interested in 'saving our village inheritance and upholding the traditional Right of Sanctuary by stopping the sale of Sentry House for redevelopment' to attend. The notice was signed by Thomas Hewitt Chairman.

As she finished reading the poster, she caught the last words of what the man called Tom had been saying.

" . . . we're growing stronger all the time. But there's not a lot we can legally do to stop the house going — I saw my solicitor yesterday and it seems we can just lodge a protest, and that's all."

"Hard." Ted polished a glass thoughtfully.

"Wrong, you mean; when you think how long Sentry's been here, and how we've all benefitted from those Rights of Sanctuary over the years, what with old Sir Bart letting the place be used for all the village festivities, using the grounds as allotments, allowing Charlie and Nip and their families to camp here, and so on — well, I tell you, it's wrong to let the place get into the hands of a damned developer now."

There was passion in the words and, fascinated, but suddenly uneasily tense, Robin watched the young farmer take a long pull at his beer and then light up an ancient pipe, one brawny arm extended along the counter as if he were part of the old oak structure himself.

So feelings ran high about Sentry House . . . she finished the last sip of her drink and surreptitiously pulled her chair deeper into the shadowy corner.

Ted nodded down the counter towards Charlie and Nip, still arguing noisily over their refilled tankards. "Made up your minds, then, you two? What d'you plan to do?"

"Stayin'," said Charlie shortly. Nip glared and moved back a step impatiently.

"I'm fer going, sooner the better. I tell 'ee, I've heard that things are gonna happen, any moment, about the House . . . "

Ted grinned. "Had your ear to the ground, eh, Nip? Well, what d'you say to all this then, Tom? These two have been arguing and scrapping for weeks now."

The farmer turned and stared at the two gypsies as they lolled against the counter some feet away from him. He took the pipe from his mouth and said slowly, clearly measuring each word, "The old days are dead and gone, Charlie, and we've got to move with the times. But not without a fight, I can tell you, and that's for sure. If the house *is* sold, you won't have a home any more; it's as simple as that."

Charlie scowled and looked thunderous. "But I've got those ole Rights to protect me! Sanctuary, that's what I'm claiming, Sanctuary, like in the old days. I've lived in that there summer-house and my 'van for ten year or more now, I ain't amoving, and that's flat! And anyone who tries to make me will be in trouble."

A loud outburst of general argument met his words, and with a resigned grin, the farmer turned away from the bar, approaching the fire and Robin's shadowy corner.

She felt keen eyes glancing her way and drew back, hoping not to get involved in conversation. She was suddenly nervous of having her identity revealed; from all she had heard tonight she could well be the pig-in-the-middle of a particularly unpleasant village upset.

"Evening." Again the blue eyes came her way, and reluctantly she knew she had to meet them.

"Good evening." Smiling dismissively,

she took a notebook from her bag and studied it deliberately, but he wouldn't be put off.

"You're a stranger here?"

She glanced up unwillingly and caught his attractive smile. "Er, yes, I'm staying for a couple of days."

"You've picked good weather. Cold, but it's dry, for a change."

"Yes."

He smiled, more determinedly, his ordinary face lighting up with pleasantness, and she thought, unexpectedly, 'Why, he's really quite good looking — '

"Haven't I seen you before?"

Coldly, she parried his assumed friendliness. "I bet you say that to all the female visitors!"

An expression of recognition slid down his face, and before she could add sharply that she thought it most unlikely that they had ever met before, he said quickly, "Of course! The white Mini — Sorry I had to make you back up — there wasn't a space for a good two hundred yards the way I'd just come . . . " Now he was smiling in a decidedly friendly manner, glancing at the empty chair beside her with obvious intent. "May I sit down? I'm Thomas Hewitt. I farm here in the village."

Dumbly she nodded. She'd guessed it, of course; the chairman of the Keep Sanctuary Open party. Desperately, she struggled for words that would be polite but not tell him who she was. He was looking at her, clearly waiting for an introduction.

Robin grasped her self-control firmly and reminded herself that she was twenty-four years of age, sophisticated and experienced in such matters as easy pick-ups; really, anyone would think she had become a village yokel herself, the way she was behaving! All that was needed was some light chatter to cover the awkward moment; no need to say who she was — nothing could be easier.

"As you're a local bigwig, Mr Hewitt — " She nodded teasingly towards the poster on the wall, " — wouldn't it be a good thing to do something about sticking a sign up at that wretched cross-roads? No wonder I snapped at you like that this morning — I thought I was lost in the wilderness!"

"But you got here in the end, I'm glad to say."

She saw appreciation in his smile and rallied herself further to keep the conversation going without giving away any information that might cloud the issue. In the middle of a discussion of the wet winter, both here and in London, and the alarming results upon the countryside, Jean, the landlord's wife, came into the bar with a laden tray.

"Evening, all. Hallo, Tom — how's Sarah? I heard Janet say she'd been a bit off-colour."

Tom rose immediately, and Robin heard a deeper warmth enter his voice. "She's better, thanks, Jean. Just a sniffle. Making great plans for the party on Saturday, I can tell you."

"Oh, that's good. Twenty of them, can you imagine it? Glad you decided to hold it in the village hall instead of my back room — I don't want jelly and crisps all over my new carpets, thank you!"

Robin seized the opportunity to leave her corner and sit at the bar. "Thanks, Mrs Mullins, I'll have it here. The soup smells fabulous."

She was very aware of Tom Hewitt as she settled herself at the long counter; but he remained by the fireplace, smoking his noisome pipe and drinking a second pint of beer. Robin, as she ate, thought curiously about Sarah who hadn't been well, but was looking forward to the party on Saturday — his daughter, obviously. Strange to realise he was married. She caught herself up savagely; why on earth shouldn't he be married? And what was it to her, anyway? But somehow she'd thought he was single, from the way he'd been chatting her up, from the look in his honest blue eyes . . . disconcerted, and ashamed of it, she realised she had even hoped he *was* single.

The evening wore on, growing busier and noisier, and by the time Robin had finished the beef curry and asked for a black coffee, the bar was quite full.

She sat there, a stranger in what was virtually a foreign country, warm, well-fed and content, and more than a little surprised at her own reactions to the place and the situation.

The pub was smoky and humming with voices, but it had an atmosphere which overlaid everything else. Dreamily, Robin tried to visualise the generations of villagers who had stood in this narrow bar, airing their grievances, gossiping, courting . . .

The association of ideas pulled her up sharply, and she stopped her day-dreaming with an ironic grin, wondering what had happened to make London-bred Robin change into a village girl, aware only of the blue eyes in the corner, which constantly sought her out, over and around the bodies that jostled the bar in such jocular fashion.

She concentrated hard on the happenings of the day and on what she must do tomorrow. In spite of the uneasiness that had assailed her upon seeing Tom Hewitt's poster, Robin liked the idea of spending more time in Sennerton. The meal Jean Mullins had produced had been simple but good, and the glances that fell her way were friendly. She felt more than a little ashamed of her hostile attitude earlier in the day.

Tobacco smoke wreathed slowly around the ancient black beams and spiralled around spluttering candles, and the voices droned on and on, laughter frequently breaking out above the loud chatter. Jean was pulling pints nonstop, and shouting over her shoulder, "Ted, hurry up with that coffee, can't you? I need some help — only got one pair of hands, you know . . . "

Robin discovered that Tom Hewitt had pushed through the crowd to stand beside her, his tankard empty and the pipe stuffed away in his jacket pocket. He grinned down at her, raising his voice to make it heard. "I'm off now — nice meeting you. Er — will you be here again tomorrow? I usually come in at the same time in the evening . . . "

Meeting his direct gaze, she thought, half-amused, half-touched, *good heavens, he wants to make a date!* To her own surprise, she said demurely, "Oh yes, I shall be here; I'll look forward to seeing you then, Tom."

The name slipped out and she bit her lip. The expression on his face was one of surprise, mixed with pleasure, and she told herself quickly that she shouldn't have encouraged him; what did she think she was doing, making a date with a shabby farmer in a one-eyed country village? But, in spite of herself she warmed to his smile as he said enthusiastically, "That's great! But I — er — I still don't know your name — "

The question hung in the hot, smoky air and she was uneasily trying to decide just how much she should tell him, when once again the door flew open and a man entered.

The newcomer was greeted with welcome shouts from his cronies clustered around the bar, and Tom involuntarily glanced over his shoulder. Then he turned back to Robin, grinning broadly. "The village news-gatherer . . . he doesn't miss a trick, I can tell you! No one's reputation is safe with Nick Harris."

Robin was relieved that the moment of truth regarding her name had been bypassed. She smiled and, to cover the slight pause, said lightly, without really thinking what she was saying, "I hope he hasn't discovered anything about me!"

"We'll soon see. Well, Nick, what's the latest news? Come on, you old ruffian, we're all ears!"

At Tom's words an expectant hush fell

on the crowded bar, and all heads turned towards Nick Harris. A small, bent man, with an eager expression on his tanned face, he had the charismatic presence of a true performer and, upon finding himself the centre of attention, quickly seized the opportunity to shine.

He nodded briefly at Jean. "Evenin', Missis. Pint, please. Well now . . . I've got some *real* news, so I have. Pin back yer lug-holes! A person I know — no names, no pack-drill — just happened to hear of a certain telephone conversation — "

Here the whole bar broke into mocking laughter and friendly catcalls. "We know the lady, Nick!"

"That's no lady — that's his wife!"

"Mrs Harris don't run the village shop *and* the gossip circle fer nothing . . . "

Undeterred, Nick took a long swig of beer, then wiped his mouth with his sleeve, and expertly timed his next words.

"As I was saying — if you'll allow me to finish — this 'ere telephone call was made by Mr Guy Devenish, who we all know is the owner of Sentry House, even though he lives in foreign parts and don't bother about the old place. *Well — "*

"Get on with it, Nick."

"*Well!* If I can get a word in edgeways — what I'm sayin' is this — that call said that someone is comin' down to Sennerton to look at the house and make arrangements for it to be bulldozed down. An' that's the truth."

"Sentry House knocked down? *Never . . . "*

Nick licked his lips and looked around him triumphantly. "And, what's more, this chap who's planning it all — Ford, his name is, Robin Ford, if I've got it right — is actually here . . . *now.*"

A hush fell and heads turned, looking first at one another, then gradually surveying the whole bar, searching for a strange face. Searching, Robin realised with a heart beating faster than usual, for her . . .

Having dropped his bombshell, Nick Harris returned to his beer and more intimate conversations with those nearest to him, but the seed of suspicion was sewn. Even Tom's face, Robin saw, with a feeling of dismay, had become cold and tense. He, too, was looking around the bar, searching for the traitor.

She wondered what would happen if she suddenly stood up and announced, 'I'm Robin Ford'; the thought struck panic into her, and she experienced an urgent need to get away before she was discovered.

Abruptly, she got to her feet. "I — I think I'll go up to my room and have an early night. I'm a bit weary — all that driving, you know . . . and the country air . . . well, goodnight, Tom."

He turned at once, and the warm smile had returned. "Of course. Well — till tomorrow then . . . "

She edged herself away from the bar counter, pushing past slowly yielding bodies until she reached the door leading to the stairs. Escape was within reach, and thankfully she grasped the handle.

Then Ted Mullins' voice range out, loud and clear, over the chattering customers. "Aren't you going to have your coffee, Miss Ford?" And because she didn't answer immediately, repeated her name, louder, clearer . . .

"Miss Ford. *Miss Ford* — "

The silence that fell then was complete. Dazed, Robin knew she could have heard the proverbial pin drop; but only for a few seconds. Then it seemed that all hell was let loose as voices shouted, angry, menacing voices that made her tremble. Every face in the bar was staring at her; every eye focused upon her as she stood there by the half-open door.

One voice rang out above the others, and a tall bulky figure pushed forward to confront her. She gasped at the hatred in his face, the harsh dislike of his rough voice.

"So you're the one! Robin Ford, eh? You think you're gonna pull the old house down, do you? Well, my fine lady, you'd best think again . . . 'cause we won't let you get near Sentry House, ain't that so?" Charlie threw a demanding glance around the bar and the response was overwhelming. Robin realised, with a sinking feeling, that she was quite alone in this angry company, the traditional spy in the enemy camp.

But the situation sparked off her determination not to be brow-beaten; suddenly her usually cool head returned, and unabashed, she faced the muttering crowd. "Now look — just let me tell you exactly what's happening. Calm down, can't you? There's nothing definite planned for the future yet. And I'm only trying to do my job — "

She was shouted down immediately. Threats arose out of inflamed passions and drink-befuddled minds. "Get back where you come from — "

"We'll run you out of the village, my girl!"

She stiffened, her professional pride upset. "I've come here to do a job, and nothing's going to stop me! Who do you all think you are? Some self-contained smug little community that's better than the rest of the world? If you only knew how pathetic you really are . . . I shall make a report on Sentry House, just as I've been instructed to do, and that's that!"

Another voice rose over her last words, a voice she had thought increasingly charming and pleasant. Until now. "So that's who you are — a snooper! No wonder you didn't want to tell me your name."

Tom Hewitt's face was tight and contemptuous. The words barked out at

41

her with such ferocity that instinctively she took a step backwards and felt her spirit quail. She had thought he was an admirer, a friend, he'd been so attentive, so nice . . .

"Tom!" Her voice broke as she said his name, not believing he could have changed so quickly, that he could be so unfair without hearing the true facts of the matter.

But he left her in no doubt at all of his opinion. "Take my advice and go back to London — and quickly. You're not welcome here, Miss Ford. *Miss Robin Ford* . . . "

The sneer in his voice brought angry colour to her cheeks, but before she could find a smart answer he had turned and pushed his way to the bar door, disappearing into the night.

The grumbling villagers gave her last baleful glances, and then returned to their tankards and their conversations. Salvaging what was left of her pride and courage, Robin slipped out of the room, going thankfully to her quiet bedroom, where an electric fire glowed in the uncurtained darkness, and pale moonlight showed her that the bed had been invitingly turned down.

She shut the door behind her with immense relief. What a terrifying experience that had been, and how wonderful it was to be safe and quiet, in this little haven of warmth of peace.

With a splintering crack that made her heart race anew, a stone came hurtling through the window, and glass showered the carpet. A cold wind roared through the ugly gap the stone had made, seeming to freeze all the blood in her veins.

She stood as if mesmerised, staring at the broken window and the heavy, sharp-sided stone, as the unwelcome truth hit home. Catching her breath, she discovered she was shaking. Who, here in quiet, innocent Sennerton, hated her enough to throw such a symbol of violence through her window; such an undoubted warning of danger still to come?

3

SOMETHING white lay beside the stone — Robin bent and picked it up, a piece of tattered paper with some words scribbled in blue biro. With shaking hands she smoothed it out and took it to the bedside lamp. The light fell on the smudgy words so that they leaped off the soiled paper, almost hitting her with their sharp and unwelcome impact.

YORE IN DANGER LOOK OUT

Her knees felt weak and she collapsed on the bed, staring at the message. Ridiculous, she told herself this wasn't the scene of murder chases or bank robberies, it was a sleepy Devon village where nothing ever happened.

But then she recalled the history of Sentry House, and knew grimly that she was wrong. Many violent things must have happened in and around the village in days past — criminals and refugees alike had fled to Sentry House to find help there, hadn't they? Well, she would be there herself tomorrow, but she knew she was more likely to find difficulties than the traditional refuge from danger.

Bleakly, she stared down at the paper. YORE IN DANGER. The writing was clumsy and ill-formed. A child's joke? But she didn't know any children . . . and the message had come forcefully, at a vital time, when she was still smarting under the unkind and threatening comments of the mob downstairs. No, it wasn't a joke, she decided wretchedly. It was a warning, and one she would do well to heed.

Pulling herself together, she went to bed, but not, for some time, to sleep. When at last she did relax, it was to dream of an empty mansion and men with relentless eyes hunting her down the long, lonely corridors.

In the morning, however, her natural optimism re-asserted itself and she was able to smile faintly as she recalled the animosity in the bar the previous evening. Tempers ran high, of course, when drink and good causes took control. Perhaps today things wouldn't seem so bad after all — but then she remembered the warning on the scrap of paper and her smile froze. The words ran around in her thoughts as she dressed and then went downstairs for her breakfast.

LOOK OUT . . .

It took a determined slice of self-confidence to brave the stares of Ted and his wife in the bar and to say airily, "Good morning. Yes thanks, I slept very well. Mmmm, egg and bacon would be fine."

While she waited, she went to the window to inspect the day. "*Cold but dry*." Tom Hewitt's voice echoed in her head, and she told herself sharply that it was a pity he had turned out to be no more than an ill-mannered petty, countrified bore. Why bother to think of him? Soon she would be back in London, among her own colleagues and friends, away from stuffy prejudices and parochial attitudes.

Jean brought the tray to the table in the window, her face plainly curious as she asked, "Are you staying another night, Miss Ford? I know you booked for two but we wondered — "

Wondered if I would take the hint and go! thought Robin acidly. Aloud,

46

she answered casually, with only a hint of smugness, "Yes, please. I'm carrying on just as we arranged."

Jean didn't comment, just left the room quickly, and Robin heard a quick, inaudible buzz of words in the kitchen. She attacked her breakfast grimly. Let them talk. Let them threaten. She would see the job through and be damned to them all . . .

As she stepped out of the front door into the cold, bright morning, she saw faces at front cottage windows hastily retreating and curtains twitching. A van delivering milk drew away in a swirl of dust as she approached, making her jump back quickly to the safety of the narrow pavement. Once she thought she saw Bert Woodall's distinctively battered hat inside a high-hedged garden, but he had disappeared by the time she reached the hedge and glanced over.

Robin took a deep breath and marched on towards Sentry House. So no one wanted to acknowledge her presence in the village. She looked around quickly; a dog sniffed the bole of the big oak tree on the village green, and a mop-haired boy slouched idly in the shadows cast by the towering greystone wall.

Squaring her shoulders, she threw off the unfriendly atmosphere and walked briskly up the drive towards Sentry House. She would get the survey job done, see a few local contractors about the possibility of using them in the first stages of the intended demolition, before Derek brought down his fleet of monster bulldozers and earth-movers, and then she would drive back to London first thing tomorrow, to her own home and her own world. It would be an enormous relief to get this wretched place out of her system.

Robin smiled in pleasant, if grim, anticipation, as she rehearsed what she would say to Derek next time she saw him.

An ominous sound made her glance back. The drive was empty, just a length of weedy gravel with Bert Woodall's cabbage patch on one side and a shabby caravan parked beside an ancient, timbered summerhouse on the other. From a clump of thick bushes a donkey's wail arose and Robin grinned with relief.

She was imagining things. She'd heard Chatterbox rustling in the undergrowth, that was all. Stupid to think it was somebody following her.

The old house looked bigger and emptier in the winter sunlight and she had to steal herself to go inside. The silence in the musty interior reminded her abruptly of her experience the previous evening and, even as she scolded herself, she was aware that her pulse rate was quickening. Horror stories, indeed! "Get on with the job and forget the unfriendly village, the threats, the warning on that bit of paper," she muttered, intent on stiffening her weakening resolve, as she got out her notebook.

LOOK OUT

Her heart raced and she stopped abruptly at the top of the huge, sweeping staircase. A step. Definitely a footstep. She stared behind, nerves tightly strung, eyes raking the empty hall below. No one there. She told herself grimly not to be ridiculous. It had all been so much talk last night, no one really meant her any harm.

She recovered her control, and then

the pen flew and the notes and the measurements went down on record mercifully blanking out the uneasy fears. Lovingly, she examined the panelling along the first floor gallery; once it had been beautiful, and it hurt to think of a bulldozer pounding that wonderful craftsmanship to powder.

As she ascended the stairs leading to the second floor, something definitely banged, far below, and she nearly jumped out of her skin. She grumbled at herself out loud — anything to break the menacing silence.

"Get a grip on yourself girl!" She was angry at giving way to her over-worked imagination, and resisted the urge to go back to the head of the servants' staircase and look down. "There's nothing there, no one coming up. Carry on with what you're supposed to be doing, for heaven's sake . . . "

Her writing grew uneven and shaky, but she persisted and soon once again became engrossed in her work, quite forgetting the fear that still nudged the edge of her busy mind. Slowly but surely the house revealed itself to her in all its neglected glory, and her pen continued to fly over the pages.

"Second floor rooms in poor condition, woodworm in a couple of places, door lintels rotting. Plumbing suspect. Window frames dangerous." She paused at a small bolted door at the end of a winding corridor and pulled determinedly at the rusty bolt. Reluctantly it gave way and the door creaked open, revealing a dark flight of steps. "Attics, I suppose — oh well, here we go."

The steps felt insecure and creaked loudly as she climbed up. Light from a broken skylight showed her a long space filled with forgotten boxes and broken furniture. A mouse skittered across the rubbish-laden bare boards and for an instant she felt returning panic.

Thankfully she wrote the last comment in the notebook and turned away from the cobwebs and the litter, hurrying back towards the little staircase. Relief flooded in on her. Now she could get out of this dirty, decaying, haunted old house . . .

She had her foot poised for descent when, without warning, the door at the foot of the stairs shut with a sharp bang.

Plunged into darkness, Robin stopped, heart abruptly hammering, but quickly recovered enough to tell herself it must be the wind. Then unbelievably, she heard the rusty bolt being fastened on the other side of the door. She stepped back, chilled to the marrow and full of fear.

Someone had shut her in. She was locked here, in this filthy attic. She could be here for ever . . . so someone really did mean to harm her. It wasn't a joke, the warning had been genuine enough —

YORE IN DANGER LOOK OUT

Robin opened her mouth and screamed.

The thin cry echoed around her head, but couldn't penetrate the mass of stone and timber that surrounded her imprisoned body. It bounced off the sides of the staircase and came back to her own ears as a helpless, pitiful protest that no one outside would ever hear. Shock sent her racing down the creaking wooden steps to pound, panic-striken, at the bolted door.

"Let me out! Let me out!"

She could hardly believe it when there

was a grating sound of the bolt being withdrawn. The door swung outwards and she caught her breath, body tense, her whole being concentrated on the fear of who was waiting for her . . .

A face looked up into hers; a merry, mischievous face with laughing black eyes and uptilted mouth. Strong features, slightly familiar, a puckish look to the ears and untidy, jet-dark hair — the mop-haired urchin she had vaguely noticed in the village!

He grinned unconcernedly at her stunned expression. "Caught you, didn't I? My golly, you didn't 'arf scream!"

Anger suddenly took hold of her and she lashed out wildly, sweating palm catching the boy's cheek in a stinging blow. "You little devil! How dare you play tricks like that!"

Immediately, she regretted her impulsive reaction. The boy turned away, the expression on his face changing abruptly. Gone in an instant was the wicked enjoyment, the laughing delight; instead, he became sullen and defensive. He slouched away, staring out of the cracked window at the end of the corridor.

"Didn't mean no 'arm."

She followed him, unable at first to catch his mumbled words. Anger and shock still raced within her, but she tried hard to control them with humour, something about the boy's bowed shoulders making her wish she hadn't been so quick-tempered.

"If I'd been old and grey you could have given me a heart attack, you know!"

He hunched himself closer to the wall and muttered, "Well, you aren't. And you didn't — "

"But I might — if you ever do things like that again."

She was quite recovered now and it was strangely important to make friends with the boy. He didn't answer, so she put a tentative hand on his shoulder. "Cat got your tongue?"

That did it. The shaggy head turned and the dark eyes stared into hers. Sombre at first, then slowly, as she smiled reassuringly back at him, they livened once again into that merriness that had enraged her so at first. "Sorry, Miss. Didn't mean to scare you. On'y a joke — ."

"I forgive you. Millions wouldn't, but I do. What's your name?"

He puffed himself up, standing tall and cocky beside her. "Manny, short for Manful. Manful Lee, that's me."

"Robin Ford. How do you do, Mr Lee?" Solemnly she held out her hand, amused by the puzzled look on his mobile face.

"Eh? Oh! Howdy!" And he shook her hand until she winced and pulled it away.

"You don't know your own strength, Manny. I'm just a poor, weak female, treat me gently, will you?"

"Sure!" He was grinning now as if they had been friends for ever. Robin nodded towards the staircase, twenty yards away.

"I've finished up here — coming down?"

"Yeah. I on'y came to see you were all right. Keep an eye on you, like."

She paused at the head of the stairs, intrigued. "Really? That was nice of you. But why — ?"

"Got my note, didn't you?"

"So it was *you* last night!" Suddenly she roared with laughter, a weight mercifully lifting from her shoulders.

"Good, wasn't it? Jest like on telly, warning you — on'y hope ole man Mullins don't know it was me. Zoom, it went through the window like a rocket, first go!"

"I promise not to tell."

"Thanks, Miss."

Robin felt drawn to the boy in some inexplicable way. She wasn't fond of children, she'd had enough of them when, as an orphaned eight-year old, she had gone to live with her aunt in north London. The rowdy brood of cousins had been demanding and difficult for a fastidious child to cope with. Now she listened to Manny's non-stop chatter as they went downstairs together, only half attending to him, a portion of her mind abruptly transported back to those unhappy childhood years.

" . . . got to help with the scrap with Dad and Uncle, see, so I didn't get the school bus. Hid behind the wall till it had gone, that's when you saw me . . . "

Aunt Margaret had been kind in her rushed, brusque way, but Robin had needed a different sort of life and those years had proved hard going. She seldom cared to think back, but now, with Manny's voice piercing her churning subconscious, she realised abruptly that those difficult early relationships had made her into the woman she now was — ambitious, insecure, fighting shy of anything other than surface friendships.

She didn't concentrate on Manny's glib patter until his silence alerted her. They stood uncertainly outside the old house, and she knew he was waiting for her next move. Knew, too, that the wrong word could make or break this strange new relationship so suddenly and unexpectedly thrust upon her.

Looking down at the boy's watching face, she said gently, "I need a guide, Manny — someone who can show me the grounds. Like to apply for the job?"

The brilliant smile flashed out and immediately he was off swaggering ahead of her, lifting a trailing ivy tendril so that it wouldn't swing back into her face. "Sure! Come on — this way!"

4

MANNY proved an excellent guide, his squirrel-like hoard of local and village hear-say opening her eyes to many aspects of the grounds that she would never have discovered for herself.

They walked beside the boundary fence and he pointed out last year's magpie's nest in a tall, straggling Scots pine.

"Lots of birds and animals here, Miss — used to get otters, higher up the river."

"Oh, how lovely — "

"Don't any longer. River's polluted, banks collapsing."

"That's sad; such beautiful creatures."

Manny wiped his nose on his sleeve and looked sideways at her. "Won't *ever* come back, not with all this dug up to make playgrounds and golf courses and swimmin' pools . . . "

"Hmmmm." Robin took the pointed

comment calmly. Of course, she sympathised about the otters, but reminded herself that she was doing a job and couldn't afford to be over-sentimental. Then she remembered that conservation was, indeed, important, and wondered uneasily if Derek had considered that aspect of things. She looked at Manny as they ended their walk, finishing up on the gravel drive again.

Suddenly she said, "When you sent that note, you said it was a joke — ."

He nodded. "'S'right."

"But — you must have heard something; someone saying that I was here, that they didn't want me in the village?"

"Yeah! Dad and Uncle, old Nick Harris too, oh, lots of 'em, all said you'd better watch it."

Something turned chill inside her. "So it wasn't really a joke; the note, I mean?"

He considered. "No — o. S'pose someone might have a go at you if they got really nasty; Uncle Nip, now, he's got a proper temper, he has — but you needn't worry, Miss — I'll protect you."

She could only smile at his impish

ferocity and pride, even though his words brought a return of the old apprehension. Manny's eyes drew hers back to him.

"That's my Mum there; come and say hallo."

Robin looked into Britannia Lee's suspicious eyes. A heavy, handsome woman with gold earrings and workworn hands, Brit nodded briefly at Manny's introduction.

"Oh ah, come about the house, have you? Gonna knock it down? I warns you, lady, keep off." The hawklike eyes were coldly stern and Robin's assurance slipped.

"I'm simply here to look at the place, Mrs Lee. There's nothing definitely planned about its future yet . . . "

"Bad things happen to folks who interfere where they'm not wanted."

Robin held her tongue and waited, feeling the tension grow. Grossly, Manny said, "Miss here ain't interferin', on'y doing her job, Mum."

"Shut yer mouth. I warns you, lady, there's words and curses can bother the likes of you." Brit stalked into the dimness of the summerhouse and shut the door with a bang.

Manny said feebly, "She's terrible down about us moving. Come and see the ole moke."

Chatterbox stared balefully, wrinkled mouth chewing stringy weeds. Robin looked at the creatures skinny frame and lack-lustre eyes and felt depression heap even more heavily on her shoulders. What would happen to Chatterbox if the gypsies had to go?

Manny read her thoughts. "Too old fer the road," he said sadly. "Ole moke'll go to the knacker, I reckon."

Robin took a grip on herself. Firmly she looked at her watch. "Well, Manny, my lad, thanks for your help. I've got things to do now. See you again, I'm sure — "

"But I gotta protect you. Like I said. Gotta be with you — "

"Well, perhaps later. Sorry, Manny, but I really must write up my report. I'll see you around."

"But I gotta . . . "

She fled before matters got out of hand. Turning out of the drive she glanced back and saw him scuffing the gravel drive fifty yards away; as she entered the pub door he was propping up the tree on the green. Clearly, he took his protecting role very seriously. Smiling wryly, strangely touched by his devotion, she went to her room to write her notes into a lucid report.

A knock on the door an hour later coincided with the end of the job. "Come in."

Jean looked wide-eyed and impressed. "Mr Devenish's in the bar, Miss Ford — says would you go down?"

"Mr Devenish!" Robin put away her papers and wondered how he had run her to earth. "Thanks, Jean — tell him I'll be down in a minute, would you?"

In the bar she saw he was surrounded by curious villagers, but he stood up and came towards her immediately. She felt surprise and animosity reaching out at her from the bystanders, and her determination to see the job through grew as a result.

"Hallo, Mr Devenish — I didn't expect to see you here . . . "

"Why not? It's my stamping ground, after all. Good to meet you, Miss Ford."

He took her hand in his and she warmed to the kindly expression on his extremely good-looking tanned face. "Can I get you a drink? And what about a bite to eat? I'm visiting friends of my uncle's, and thought I'd probably find you here — not exactly five-star, but I believe it's comfortable."

Robin thought he was most attractive, with a friendly, if decidedly worldly, manner. Certainly he was easy to talk to — and it was flattering to realise he had come looking for her. After last evening's experience, her morale was pleasantly boosted by the fact. Over bread and cheese and Jean's home-made chutney they talked freely, and Robin found herself responding easily to his undeniable charm.

He asked her about herself — how she came to be in the property business, what hobbies she had, whether she lived near her family — and it seemed to Robin that his words, not merely curious, but apparently containing genuine interest, searched out many things hidden deep within her, things rarely, if ever, taken out for self-examination.

Suddenly uninhibited, she told him of Aunt Margaret's busy family, and her own rather solitary existence in it; of her neat, comfortable flat in Ealing, of her circle of friends and her obsession with historical houses; and then, colour mounting high, realised she had revealed more of herself in one short hour than a casual acquaintance such as this had any right to know.

But Guy — " . . . call me Guy, please," he had said right at the start of their conversation — appeared to be able to read her thoughts, for he said quietly, as she ran out of words and looked foolishly at her empty plate, "I'm honoured that you should talk to me like this, Robin. Pretty girls like you usually only chatter about superficial things. I've enjoyed the privilege of listening to you."

With an effort she directed the conversation back into business channels. "I like your old house, Guy, and I can see why half the village is up in arms about losing it."

He smiled. "I know what you mean, of course, but you must realise I wasn't born here; I never loved it as my uncle did. In fact, I wouldn't care if I never saw it again! That's why I'm determined that the sale must go through — and as quickly as possible."

Strangely, his uncaring words irritated her. "Well, of course, I see all that, but a lot of people depend on Sentry House and its grounds and privileges, and the bottom will fall out of their small worlds if it goes . . . "

"*When* it goes, you mean. Come now, Robin, I'm a business man, I can't afford to indulge in such sentimentality!"

She looked up indignantly. "Even so, one can't just push people around!"

The sunburned skin crinkled attractively around his deepset eyes. "Hey, whose side are you on? I thought you were working for the developers, not the village do-gooders!"

She met his smile levelly, forcing herself to acknowledge the truth of what he said. "You're right, of course. Stupid of me — I'm not usually emotional about my work."

Her head swam. The events of the day had somehow unbalanced her; first Manny, with his reminders of her childhood, then Guy with his gift for listening, and now . . . she gulped and avoided his eyes.

A strong, warm hand suddenly covered hers as they lay in her lap. "I know what you mean; business often conflicts with humanity. And you're a sensitive woman, concerned with other people — don't change Robin, you're fine as you are."

The quiet words brought the colour to her cheeks again. "Thank you, Guy; that's the nicest compliment I've ever had . . ."

He glanced at his watch. "I've got to see my solicitor this afternoon — look, how about having dinner with me in Exeter later this evening? We've only just started to get to know each other — please, Robin?"

"I'd love to." Something warm and happy grew inside her.

"Splendid! Let's say about seven at the White Stag, near the Cathedral — that suit you?"

"Fine." She watched him leave, followed by enquiring faces which all turned back to her as the door slammed. Ignoring the curious eyes she slipped out of the bar and returned to her room.

In the quietness of the afternoon she went over her report again, seeing in her mind's eye the magnificence of the old house, the potential beauty of the neglected grounds. Suddenly, she laid down her pen and relaxed into deep thought, the imagines and feelings she had experienced since she arrived in Sennerton re-running through her mind like a kaleidoscope of colour and emotion; and out of the inner confusion slowly arose a nugget of truth which she was quite unable to deny. She hated the mere idea of knocking down Sentry House and redeveloping the site.

Chalets, bars, putting-greens and a swimming pool full of chlorinated water and noisy people where once the rare and beautiful otters had swum and bred? *Never* . . .

With astonishment, she came to the wretched conclusion that she was a hypocrite, working against the standards of her own conscience. What was she to do? Getting up, she wandered to the window and stared into the lowering light of the winter afternoon; her eyes lighted on Manny, sitting on the milk platform opposite. Ridiculously, she felt immediately guilty — poor boy, had he had any lunch?

Grabbing her jacket and bag, she ran downstairs, pausing to buy a bag of crisps from Ted as she went. Outside, she called across the green, "Come on, protector, I've brought food for the troops — "

Manny caught the bag expertly. "My golly, bacon flavour, that's my favourite — thanks!"

"I thought we'd go and find a builder who could do a spot of clearing up if I need him — do you know someone?" So much better to do something positive than sit and mope, she thought numbly; soon enough she would have to examine her conscience and come to a final decision, but for the moment it was necessary to keep moving and avoid the moment of truth.

"Sure, Tony Powell, not far." Manny strode beside her, chewing noisily, rustling the paper bag. "Is this your car? My golly, clean, isn't it? Can I drive, Miss?"

"Certainly not. Get in and don't spill crisps everywhere."

It didn't take long to get to Tony Powell's yard outside the village and to have a quick word with the young builder. Honest eyes met her with disconcerting directness. Yes, he'd be glad to give her a price for the initial work, if required.

"We need something new in Sennerton," he said emphatically. "A holiday place like that would bring in new jobs, new opportunities. There's some against, I daresay, knowing the village and all the old folks, but I look at it like this — progress brings change and we've all got to live . . . "

Robin bought Manny a cream tea later in the afternoon, wondering at the keen enjoyment she experienced, watching him push scone after scone piled with jam and crusty, golden cream down his voracious gullet. She hadn't known that kids could be so much fun.

Reluctantly, she forced him to go home when they returned to Sennerton. "I'll be O.K. now, Manny; Mr Devenish will look after me this evening. And I expect I'll see you before I leave tomorrow."

He looked deflated. "Promise?"

"Of course."

"Well, all right — but look out. You never know what's round the corner," he warned chillingly, as she dropped him off at the drive leading to the house.

At the pub she made herself relax and have a bath before changing her clothes, anticipating a pleasant evening with Guy. Tomorrow she would be back in London. And that would mean an end to all this wretched indecision and hostility in the village; an end, too, to her own nagging doubts about her own integrity. What a relief.

Then she remembered that she ought to ring Derek and report on the day's happenings. His voice was hurried and sharp and she was shocked into dismayed silence as he said crisply over the wires, "Sorry, but you'll have to stay a bit longer, love; I've had a letter from this trouble-maker, what's he called, Thomas Hewitt, the chairman of the party that wants to save the house. Now, listen — I want you to go and see him first thing tomorrow. Turn on the charm, talk him out of his stupid idea."

Dismay filled her. "But Derek, you don't understand — "

"I understand this — the man's a farmer, a business man, isn't he? Well, appeal to his business acumen then. This is terribly important, Robin . . . "

She had a vision of his relentless face as the words went on and on.

"Damn it all, the chap can muck up the whole sale if he goes on like this. Remember, I'm relying on you to get him to change his mind . . . O.K., Robin? Fine. Cheerio, then."

The phone went dead and she replaced the receiver numbly, her mind full of churning thoughts. In her job it was quite customary to have to tackle awkward customers and she knew she could easily handle the situation. But to call on Thomas Hewitt, of all people, feeling as she did . . . she caught her breath miserably. It wouldn't be pleasant, but clearly, it must be done.

She heard the church clock strike five thirty. Tomorrow, Derek had said, but why not tonight? Now? Impossible to wait now that she had decided; much better to get the ordeal over and done with.

Impulsively, she walked across the

green towards Well Farm. The huddle of grey stone buildings seemed deserted except for a few foraging hens, and she began to hope stupidly that Tom was out — but the second pull at the bell brought footsteps along the passage. The door opened and she looked into his vivid eyes.

For a second her knees went weak, but quickly she bullied herself into her usual cool poise. She thought briefly that he looked surprised, even pleased, to see her, but then his expression became set and cold and she knew she was wrong. They were enemies. What else had she hoped for? The knowledge gave her fresh resolve.

"Good evening, Mr Hewitt. May I have a word with you, please?" The smile on her face was stiffly false, but she kept it there purposefully. Tom's eyes narrowed, and he took the pipe from his mouth slowly.

"What about?"

"Sentry House. My boss has asked me to — "

"Damn your boss! I've got nothing more to say on the matter. He's had my letter, he knows my views."

"But surely we can talk things over, negotiate?"

"No."

His stolid refusal fuelled her growing irritation. She heard her voice grow stronger and more aggressive.

"You're acting very childishly, Mr Hewitt. I'm sure we could find a mutually acceptable compromise if only you weren't so stubborn."

"Stubborn!" His face suddenly flamed and she drew back, instinctively, half afraid of the passion in his eyes. "You come here, a town girl with no knowledge of the country at all, no interest in it, and have the nerve to throw your weight about like this? You must think I'm soft in the head, talking about compromise and negotiation! I'll fight to keep Sentry House standing and that's all there is to it. On your way, Miss Ford — my land's my own and I'm fussy who comes on to it. Goodnight!"

He half shut the door, but her own anger overflowed and caught his attention.

"All right, Mr Hewitt, I'll go, but I'll

tell you this: you haven't got a hope of keeping your old house. Sentiment has no value to a business man, and money talks. So get used to the idea of Sentry being knocked down in the end! And there's one more thing I'd like to say . . . "

He forestalled her, eyes like chips of ice, voice hard and grim. "No need to say it, Miss Ford, it's quite plain from the expression on your face. You don't like me. Well, you can rest assured, the feeling's mutual. And if you ever come bothering me again you'll be in trouble. Real trouble. Just remember that.

She turned away, suddenly sick and cold. Another warning. Another threat. And from Tom Hewitt, of all people. Manny's words rang in her head — so it was true, unbelievable as it seemed; the village would resort to violence to keep Sentry House standing.

She walked to the gate, immersed in her shocked thoughts, but turned abruptly as another voice echoed behind her.

"Tom, can you come? Sarah's calling for you, her temperature's up again

. . . who's at the door, anyone important?"

"No, Janet — just a busybody, a pest, easily got rid of. Tell Sarah I'll come directly."

Robin paused, foolishly wondering if there was still a grain of friendship between them. So the child was ill — no wonder Tom was worried and emotional. Perhaps the situation might be improved if she apologised . . . ?

But the thought died instantly as Tom reached behind the door, reappearing again with a gun cradled in the crook of his arm, a bitter hatred clear on his face.

"A pest, I said, Miss Ford," he called loudly as she hesitated at the gate, staring back, hardly crediting what she saw. "And a twelve-bore doesn't bother to argue with pests and vermin. Don't let me see you here again, that's all."

Then the door slammed and Robin discovered she was trembling. Fear, once again, stalked her as she walked rapidly back to the safety of the Black Dog. Stones, curses and guns; where would it all end?

5

IT was some minutes before Robin's nerves calmed, but by the time she had returned to her bedroom and sat down by the mirror, intent on controlling her emotions, she discovered that her fears had become reactive feelings of fresh anger.

Now, as she remembered Tom Hewitt standing in the open doorway of Well Farm with a shotgun in the crook of his arm, she was furious. Slowly, however, her sense of humour asserted itself and at last she began to laugh.

The absurdity of it! He was behaving just like a liege-lord of ancient history, throwing his weight about in no uncertain terms. She outlined her lips and inspected the soft sea-green shadows emphasising her wide eyes and the thought came, unexpected and unwanted, that all he had been doing was protecting his home and letting off steam . . .

She stood up and smoothed the

shimmering, deep turquoise dress that accentuated the bright lights in her dark auburn hair, deep in thought. Then, snatching up her small gilt bag and sheepskin jacket, she went out to the Mini, cross with herself for managing to find excuses for such abominable, oafish behaviour. Well, this evening she would be with someone very different . . .

From what she knew of Guy Devenish, he was the exact opposite of Tom Hewitt. Civilised, charming. All the things a girl wanted a man to be — wasn't he?

She drove into Exeter determined to forget about Sennerton and enjoy the evening. Already her heart raced a little as she recalled Guy's appreciative looks and complimentary words at their last meeting. Undoubtedly, he was more her sort of man than that wretchedly impossible Tom Hewitt.

Eye-catching in a dark blue suit, the prematurely greying hair emphasising his suntan, Guy proved to be a good host and a most entertaining companion. Robin soon discovered that she was enjoying herself even better than she had expected. They ate a first class meal and then sat over their coffee in the lounge of the atmospheric old coaching hotel.

Mellowed by the wine, she suddenly found herself talking shop again, although it had been her intention to steer clear of the controversial subject.

"Sentry House must have been so beautiful, years ago, Guy. Even though it's only a ruin now, there's still something about it — a sort of serenity, a feeling of immense strength . . . "

She met his eyes over the table, deep pools of unfathomable grey, strikingly still and aware. Feeling foolish at her emotional outburst, she tried to pass it off lightly. "Sorry, I didn't mean to be such a bore! We don't want to talk about business, do we — let's change the subject."

"Why? You obviously feel strongly about the place."

She paused, undecided, while the image of the old house stayed in her mind. "Ye — es. I suppose I do. But I can't imagine why, I never saw it before yesterday. And after all, it's only a shell — what did you call it? A mouldering pile; yes, very apt . . . "

He laughed, but the interest still showed on his face. "That's exactly what it is to me, just an old dump that needs pushing down and redeveloping. And it'll bring me a tidy little sum, which can't be bad. I wonder what it is that I've missed about Sentry House that has so clearly caught at your vulnerable heart strings?"

"Now you're laughing at me."

His wry glance forced her into excuses. "It's just the fact that I hate to see such beautiful craftsmanship destroyed. There's some really lovely oak panelling on the first floor landing that ought to be salvaged, and those little leaded windows — well, there aren't many of those to be found nowadays, you know."

Her crisp words sounded sensible enough, but deep inside she knew that the real enchantment of the house wasn't the antique fittings, not even the grace and beauty of the actual building, but something much more intangible; an atmosphere, indescribable and haunting.

Guy's shapely eyebrows went up in mock surprise. "I can see that you're a real old-fashioned girl at heart, Robin,

beneath that elegant up-to-date veneer
. . . I love your dress, by the way. That
colour makes you look like Venus coming
out of the waves . . . "

Recovering herself she smiled blithely
enough and accepted a glass of brandy,
but his earlier words echoed around her
mind relentlessly. *Had* Sentry House
caught at her heart strings? And if so,
why? She was a town girl, as Tom
Hewitt had so vehemently reminded
her, and no ties bound her to the
countryside. Yet Sennerton, with its
rustic charm, undermined as it was
by growling conflicts and threats of
violence, had somehow seemed to cast
an entangling net around her.

As she pondered the strange problem,
her smile died, and when Guy's deep
voice said gently, "Penny for them?" she
glanced up, surprised, to catch his keen,
watchful eyes.

"Oh, this and that . . . " Unexpectedly
a sigh slipped out as she sipped the
brandy, and she was quite unprepared for
his perception as he said gently, "You're
tearing yourself apart over all this, aren't
you, Robin? I know how you must feel,

even though I can't share those feelings. But I do understand that you love Sentry House too much to have a hand in its destruction."

Initially, she had thought him no more than an attractive stranger, an astute, even ruthless, businessman; this was a new, surprising side to him, and one that touched her deeply. She blinked hard to stop the uncharacteristic tears that threatened at such unlikely understanding. "Th — thank you — "

His voice changed abruptly, and she was grateful for that, too. "Cheer up! I want this to be a happy evening, something to remember when I'm home again. Shall I tell you about my home, Robin?"

Nodding, she watched him stretch back in his chair playing with the brandy glass as his smile lifted his face into nostalgic memory. "South Africa is a great place, a different world, so vast and sunlit . . . so much to see and do. Do you know, when ever I come back to England, I'm always dismayed by the smallness of everything. So much so that usually I can't wait to get home again . . . "

He replaced the glass on the table and the smile left his face. "Mind you, this visit's been different." His voice dropped a tone and, surprised, she looked up, to see the grey eyes holding hers intently. "You see, I've met you, Robin Ford . . . and I want to see more of you. Suddenly things in England aren't small and petty any longer."

"Oh, but — " She was unsure how she felt, what she wanted. Guy smiled briefly and leaned across the table to touch her face with a light, caressing finger.

"Think about the sun on the long beaches, the animals in the bush. The sights and the smells of a new country. I know you would love South Africa, Robin."

"I daresay; it sounds very romantic."

He threw back his head and laughed. "Wrong word! South Africa is all realism, and you need to see it to understand and appreciate properly . . . " Abruptly he was serious again, his hand dropping until it covered hers on the table, warm and dominating and exciting. "Robin, when this job's over, why don't you take a holiday and come out with me? I've got a bungalow on the coast, we could have a really good time . . . I want to show you what an amazing country it is. And we could get to know each other better . . . ”

She slid her hand away, avoiding the intimate question in his deepset eyes, in his soft and insinuating words. He was moving too fast, she felt uneasy, undecided. She smiled, suddenly bright and artificial. “Sounds marvellous! But I'm afraid I'm a real stay-at-home, never been further than Paris on a day-trip when I was a teenager! But thanks for the invitation, Guy — who knows, one day, perhaps . . . ”

The spell was broken, the moment past. Sitting back, he stared into his empty brandy glass and Robin glanced thankfully at her watch. “Is that really the time? Heavens, I must be off!”

Outside in the windy Close, he kissed her cheek as he opened the door of the Mini for her. “I'll keep you up to that promise, Robin. One day, you said.”

They stared at each other through the darkness, then he stepped back. “Drive carefully. I look forward to seeing you again — and soon."

She shied from the expression in his eyes. "Thanks for a super evening, Guy. Yes, of course, we'll be in touch — "

But, as she drove away, she began wondering whether she liked him as much as her deeply aroused emotions hinted that she did. In fact, she suspected rather painfully that her enjoyment of Guy Devenish's charm and perceptive company was no more than an instinctive rebound, after Tom Hewitt's rudeness and forthright enmity.

And then, having once more conjured up thoughts of Tom, he stayed persistently in her mind as she drove back to Sennerton. The more she thought about the scene earlier in the evening, the surer she became that there must have been a legitimate cause for his rudeness, other than the vexed matter of Sentry House.

She slid into bed, still thinking hard. Tom was clearly a man of passion, outspoken and honest. When events riled him, he exploded. That had been obvious when first they met in the pub on the first evening of her visit. So wasn't it possible and feasible that something had upset him during the afternoon and that her appearance on his doorstep merely triggered off a temper ready to burst? Perhaps he hadn't really meant the beastly things he had said . . .

She remembered his daughter. Sarah could be ill again — a good reason for his anxiety and resultant bad temper. Sleepless, Robin's churning mind admitted frankly that it hated the idea of she and Tom being enemies. Must they be on such hostile terms, just because they were on opposing sides of the Sentry House issue?

And why should it matter so much to her that they were enemies, anyway? Why worry about Tom, when Guy was so likeable, attractive and — she grinned in the darkness — almost certainly hers for the taking? How difficult and complicated life was. Just before she finally drifted into exhausted sleep, she had a sudden doubt about the genuineness of Guy's offered friendship . . .

Was it possible that he had been merely chatting her up to ensure the sale of his wretched old house? That made her abruptly decide to call at Well

Farm again in the morning and enquire after Sarah — it would be nice to make up with Tom and, hopefully, end the hostility between them.

But, on the other hand, Tom had been so downright in his refusal to talk to her; "Men," she thought faintly, half asleep, "what a damned trouble they are!"

In the morning she awoke with a headache and the return of all her doubts and indecisions. After breakfast she rang Derek, unhappily aware that it would almost certainly be a difficult conversation. It was.

"What d'you mean, wouldn't talk to you? Good grief, what's come over you, Robin, you've gone all feminine and weak on me!" His sharpness hit her on the raw and made her snap back.

"I always *was* feminine — or hadn't you noticed? I suppose not, you're always too busy making money! And as for being weak, well, I challenge anyone to try and get some sense into Tom Hewitt's hard head when he's in one of his rages, male *or* female!"

"But that's exactly what I pay you for, you know," shouted Derek angrily.

"I know you do! And I've tried! It's just that he's proving extremely difficult, behaving like a spoilt child, won't talk, won't negotiate ... he's got it into his head that Sentry House must stay as it is, and that's that. Mind you, Derek, I do rather see his point: I mean, all that history, and it *has* been a beautiful place in the past, even though it's only a ruin now; you can still see the fine workmanship and the shape of the architecture ... "

"Robin!" Derek's shout was outraged. "What in God's name are you going on about? I don't care how old the damned attic is, nor if it's got mullioned windows and a monster in the attic ... all I want is to buy the place and knock it down! Now, stop yammering on like a hopeful estate agent and do as I say ... "

She ground her teeth, but said meekly. "I'm listening."

"Right. Go back to Hewitt, then, and tell him — "

"It won't be any use, he's made up his mind."

"Then make him change it, can't you?"

"Impossible! Why, I doubt if even you

could get him to do that — "

"Seems as if I'll have to try, though, doesn't it?" said Derek coldly.

"What do you mean?" She felt ashamed and furious, quite unable to make any excuses for her failure. There was a chilling silence between them, and she added unevenly, "I'm sorry, Derek . . . "

He overrode her unkindly. "You'd better come back to London, Robin, and keep an eye on things here while I deal with this Hewitt chap; that is, if you think you're still capable of handling matters — "

She took the bait fiercely. "That's rotten of you! Just because the man's impossible, there's no reason to doubt my efficiency!"

His voice softened a little. "O.K. Maybe I was a bit hard, but honestly, love, I can't imagine what's come over you."

She rang off miserably, knowing herself to be an utter failure. And Derek's last acid comment rankled; she didn't know what had come over her, either.

It didn't take long to pack her bag and settle the bill. Outside, cleaning the

Mini's windscreen before starting the journey home, the unexpected happened. A step on the road beside her made her twist around, gasping as she found herself looking into Tom Hewitt's veiled eyes.

He didn't smile, but appeared aloof and very formal. "I've come to apologise for my behaviour yesterday, Miss Ford. I said some very nasty things, I'm afraid."

Completely taken aback, Robin murmured stupidly, "I — I — well, thank you, Mr Hewitt. Perhaps I was rather rude, as well."

His grim expression never faltering, hands locked in pockets, feet astride on the frosty road, Tom bound out a grudging invitation. "I'd be very glad if you'd come in and meet Sarah. She's been asking to see you ever since I told her about you."

"Told her — about *me*?" Robin was flustered and amazed, a surge of wicked joy filling her as, abruptly, Tom's set face cracked into the vestige of a sheepish smile.

"Of course I did. It's not often one meets someone like you in Sennerton." The smile died again. "A town girl with smart clothes; independent, doing an important job, sure of herself — ."

"Not very sure of herself any longer, though," murmured Robin meekly, with a hint of laughter in her voice.

"Well — "

She could see that his bright eyes wanted to smile, but clearly his damned pride was still in control. She grinned broadly, threw the duster into the car and relocked the door. He'd made the first step towards peace, she would gladly take the second. "Lead on then, Mr Hewitt — I'm really looking forward to meeting Sarah!"

They entered Well Farm through the untidy cobbled yard, where some demure brown hens and a colourful cockerel scattered around their feet.

"Hope you don't mind coming in the back way." Tom ushered her into a large, warm kitchen.

Huge beams supported a ceiling hung with bunches of drying herbs and hams covered in clinging muslin. A vast old-fashioned black range dominated the far wall, jostled cheek by jowl with a modern electric cooker. The bare, scrubbed table, running the length of the room, told plainly of immense farm meals served over the centuries, shared between past cowmen, shepherds and the owning Hewitts, and in a battered cane chair by the fire, a mother cat licked away determinedly at her litter of mewing, blind kittens.

Robin felt a catch in her throat. This was so clearly a home, the sort of home she had never experienced in her own unadorned childhood; a home where the basic way of life held sway over the family. How wonderful to live in such a place, full of warmth and memories, amongst the good, simple things of life.

"Sarah! Janet!" Tom marched ahead and shouted down the passage leading out of a far door. He glanced back over his shoulder before he disappeared. "Sit down, she'll only be a minute."

Robin walked slowly across the stone-flagged floor, looking around and feeling the undeniable atmosphere more intently than ever before in her life. What was it spoke to her so forcibly in this old-fashioned, cluttered room? She turned as Sarah appeared.

A heart-shaped, vital face, awesomely like Tom's, with the same brilliant eyes. And below the pretty face, the cruel contrast of a crooked body contained within the grotesque frame of a wheelchair.

But there was no time for Robin to feel sorry. "Hello, Robin!" Sarah's voice was quick and impetuous, the welcome so direct and spontaneous that Robin could only blink.

"Miss Ford," corrected Tom gently, and Sarah directed her blazing smile up at him. "But *you* call her Robin, so why can't I?"

Tom turned aside quickly, striding over to the cooker, his voice stiff and awkward. "Let's have some coffee, shall we?"

A shadow behind Sarah emerged into full view. "I'll do it, Tom. Perhaps Miss — er, Ford, isn't it? — would like to go into the sitting room with Sarah. It's tidier in there." Janet's pale, hostile eyes, startled Robin, but she smiled back and held her ground.

"I'd much rather stay here, it's so warm and friendly; a lovely old room."

"As you like." Janet turned away to the

dresser and took down cups and saucers, and Tom said belatedly, "Sorry, I should have introduced you: Miss Ford, this is Janet Hopkins, my housekeeper."

It was too late to do more than smile at the middle-aged woman with the tightly drawn-back hair and unfriendly eyes. Robin did her best to cover the awkward silence that Janet's straight back emphasised. "We're being very formal, aren't we? I'm Robin and you're Tom — or we were, when we first met," she said lightly.

Tom met her gaze and allowed himself to smile a little more freely. "Right, let's take it from there, then. Come and sit here beside Sarah. She's got thousands of things to ask you, so she says."

Sarah could hardly wait to be wheeled over to the fire. "Tell me about London! Is it exciting? Noisy? Crowded? Have you seen the Queen? And the Prince and Princess Di? Oh, it must be wonderful to live up there in the middle of everything! Nothing ever happens here in dreary old Sennerton . . . "

Robin caught Tom's eye as he hovered protectively about his daughter's chair, and they smiled silently, suddenly unexpected allies. Little did Sarah know just how much happened in the village!

Robin took a deep breath and began answering the questions. She felt happily as if she had known Sarah all her life — in fact, the atmosphere of the old farm, the new-found friendliness of Tom, even Janet's undoubted hostility, were immediately influencing her thoughts and attitudes.

As she described London's hubbub of noise and events, she realised, surprised, that she would be almost sorry to leave the quiet warmth of Well Farm and return to her flat in Ealing.

The coffee cups emptied, Janet's plate of homemade flapjacks were eaten with relish, but still Sarah's untiring voice chattered on. Then, suddenly, her vivacity flagged and she shrank in her chair, closing her eyes, where exhaustion lurked. Robin felt guilty and dismay filled her.

"I've excited her too much: I should never have stayed so long — "

Tom was at the child's side in one step, kneeling down and looking into her pale face with such devotion that Robin's heart turned over. "It's not your fault," he said quickly, "she gets overtired very easily. She'll be O.K. again in a minute. I'll take her back to her own room — it's quiet there, she can sleep if she wants to." He wheeled Sarah away and Robin stood up uncertainly, meeting Janet's icy stare across the table, where she rolled past with smooth, deft hands.

"She's such a beautiful child — it's terrible that she's so handicapped. Is there any hope that she'll improve as she grows older? Medicine does such wonderful things nowadays — I would have thought perhaps a special school could help her . . . "

Janet went on rolling and the silence tightened. At last, she looked up and said flatly, "Mr Hewitt is quite capable of looking after Sarah. He doesn't need any advice from outsiders, Miss Ford."

Robin's cheeks flamed. "But I wasn't — I didn't mean — " She bit off the words and met Janet's raised eyes. Clearly, there was to be war between them. The housekeeper resented her and would make no effort to be friends. Robin turned away bitterly; why bother?

After all, she was unlikely ever to see Janet again. Purposefully, she reminded herself that today was the last time she would be in Sennerton.

Tom returned, his magnetic presence making her turn, even though she hadn't heard his step. "Sarah's going to have a nap," he said quietly. "But she wants you to come to her birthday party on Saturday — can you manage it, Robin?"

Her heart leaped and a sense of overwhelming gaiety swept through her. "I'd love to! On Saturday — oh, but — " Abruptly she remembered she was disgraced and banished, the job not completed. "I shan't be here. I'm on my way back to London, actually." Squarely and bravely she met Tom's questioning eyes, her head held defiantly high. "I've — I've been recalled. My boss is taking over from me . . . "

In the silence she saw Janet's unconcealed smile of triumph, then heard a rough tone enter Tom's voice. "I see. So he's coming himself to renew battle, is he?" Once again he looked as fierce as when he had shouted at her the previous evening. "Well, he's welcome to try — but I've got a few surprises up my sleeve yet!"

Robin's joy died a bitter death. How stupid she had been to imagine that Tom was a different person today; and yet, those moments when he had smiled at her, the warmth and care in his face as he tended Sarah — had she been so wrong then in thinking him to be a gentle, loving soul at heart?

She looked at him now and saw the grim-set face; she was a fool and had allowed herself to be misled. Tom Hewitt was a horror and that was that.

"I'll be on my way, then. Thanks for the coffee. It was lovely meeting Sarah — please thank her for the invitation and make my excuses, will you?"

He escorted her silently out of the back door and over the yard, an implacable, fierce man walking beside her, too hard and dogmatic to even talk to any longer. As she got into the Mini, she switched on a bright smile to hide the pain that seethed inside her.

"Goodbye, Tom." There was nothing else to say.

"Goodbye." He didn't even say her name.

But in the mirror, she saw him standing there in the road, watching, until she drove out of sight, leaving Sennerton behind her.

6

AS she drove along, Robin's thoughts were confused and emotional and when, half a mile out of the village, a small figure by the roadside abruptly flagged her down, she looked at Manny's hurt fact without instant recognition.

"You're going! And you didn't tell me! My golly, that's not fair — you said you'd see me this morning, you *promised*, you did!"

Robin parked the car and closed her eyes for a moment. Would it ever end? It seemed as if the village had laid a spell on her — could she ever free herself from its subtle entanglement?

"I'm sorry, Manny, really I am. But I've got so much on my mind — "

He stared in through the wound-down window, eyes huge and resentful. "You didn't even say goodbye!" His voice slid up the scale and cracked and she knew abruptly she would never forgive herself for such an omission.

"It was beastly of me. Please forgive me, Manny?"

"We-ll . . . O.K." Gradually a smile lit up his impish face and then all the familiar energy and vitality returned. "When are you coming back again, Miss?"

"Actually, I'm not coming back, Manny."

"But you said — "

"I said I was only here for a day or two. And time's up now." Robin gripped her waning self-control very tightly. It was ridiculous to let a small boy upset her so much.

He looked more woebegone than ever and she knew she had to end the painful interview quickly, for both their sakes.

"So it's goodbye for ever — my golly, who'll look after you now?"

"I'll be all right, don't you worry. You've been a super protector, Manny. I'll never forget you." She revved the engine and reluctantly he drew back from the window.

"Well, cheerio then, Miss. But — "

"Goodbye, Manny. We'll meet again

one day, I daresay." She drove off, waving energetically and pushing aside the knowledge that she would never be able to forget the look of lost trust in his darkly brooding eyes.

It was mid-afternoon when she reached London, and she made a speedy decision not to go straight away to the office. Things could surely look after themselves until the morning. She needed the comfort and seclusion of her little flat to help recover from what had been a couple of traumatic days.

The flat received her with its familiar welcome, but as the evening progressed she grew strangely restless. What was it that she lacked? Staring out of the window into the winter darkness she watched the stream of humming traffic in the road below. The sky was cloudy and thick with billowing, smog-like fog and the incessant, blurred flicker of neon lights made her eyes ache. Suddenly, she recalled Sennerton's quiet, narrow roads, the vastness of the unafflicted sky, where stars and a crescent moon had hung over the village in the peaceful evenings. She wished heartily that she was back there, and then caught her breath in amazement and dismay as the unlikely thought registered itself.

Angrily, determined to think no longer of the past, she went into the tiny kitchenette to make some coffee. But her mind obstinately went its own way, producing images of the big Well Farm kitchen, evoking the subtle smell of cooking and drying herbs, reminding her of the vital smile of a small excited girl.

"Damn!" The cup slipped from her unaware fingers, crashing on to the tile floor. Out of the blue she recalled Britannia Lee's bleak words. She rarely broke things — could this be the result of the curse the gypsy woman had warned her about? But that was absurd, she was losing her grip . . . what had Derek said? 'Going all feminine and weak.' Robin started to laugh, but discovered she had tears pricking at the back of her eyes. What had happened to her? This was no way for a career-girl, modern and independent, to carry on! Mockingly, Tom's voice echoed in her mind — a town girl with smart clothes, sure of herself . . .

Through her bewildered thoughts the door bell rang a strident note. "What now?" she muttered. "I can't take anymore!" Wearily, she flung open the door.

Manny stood there, defiant and cocky as ever, but with a hint of insecurity and apprehension in his wide, fixed grin.

"Hi!" he said, over-brightly. "I hitched up to be with you — I'm your protector, you know, and my golly, you sure need me, Miss — Mum's done her ole curse and it could start working any time now . . . "

Dismay hit her with almost physical impact. It was wicked and thoughtless of the boy to leave his home. And did Britannia truly have the power to make uncomfortable things happen? But then an unwarranted delight took hold of her, and she pulled the child into the flat, hugging him fiercely. "Oh, it's good to see you! But you really are a little devil, you know! Your poor parents must be worried stiff, not knowing where you are . . . and how on earth did you find me?"

Manny emerged tousle-headed from

her embrace, shaking himself like a wet dog, eyes wide and inquisitive, staring around him, restlessly moving from hall to lounge, into the kitchenette, back to the hall. "Easy! Slipped into the pub when ole Mullins wasn't looking and copied out what you wrote in the register! And you don't have to worry about me Mum and Dad — I left them a note," he shouted airily over his shoulder, exploring the bathroom.

"Telling them you were coming here?" Robin felt worried; she didn't want an irate Charlie on her doorstep, charging her with spiriting away his beloved son.

"Nah! Jest saying I was going on a mission; you know, like they do on telly. My golly, you got a bath *indoors*! Can I have a bath, Miss?"

"Of course, later on. Oh, do stop flitting about, Manny, and come and sit down. Take off your anorak. Are you hungry?"

"Starving!" Reluctantly he was persuaded to wash his hands and then tucked into an enormous cheese sandwich. Robin watched fondly, with hidden amusement, as he demolished the last crumb and still looked hungry.

"Manny, I'll have to get in touch with your parents, you know; tell them you're safe, and then tomorrow I'll put you on the train home."

His bright face fell, eyes staring dramatically into hers. "You mustn't do that! Don't tell 'em I'm here — Mum'll get really worked up, think you've kidnapped me, or something . . . "

"Don't be so silly! You've been watching too many adventure films. She won't think any such thing."

"Huh. You don't know my Mum. Tell you what, I'll send 'em a quick message to keep 'em happy, then I can stay up here with you. Cor, yes! I've never been to London before; take me to the Tower of London, will you Miss? The Bloody Tower?"

Torn between anxiety and a growing, unfitting mirth, Robin could only smile soothingly at her demanding guest. "You're going home tomorrow and that's it. And I'll send a telegram saying you're safe, but I won't sign it. No, stop arguing, Manny, I've made up my mind. Want an apple?"

"Don't mind." He crunched thoughtfully for a few minutes while she sat opposite him, composing a message in her mind, and imagining the effect upon sleepy Sennerton of the telegram being delivered to the Lees in their summerhouse home . . .

"I got it!" Suddenly he jumped to his feet, all glittering eyes and huge smile. "I know what to say, short, so it won't cost much. How about 'Mission accomplished. Yours faithfully, Manny Lee.' Yeah, that'd be great, then they'll know I'm safe, see, and Mum won't get the ole crystal ball out to try and find me!"

Robin's mind overflowed and she sat back weakly, laughing hilariously. "Manny, you're marvellous! Oh, you're so good for me, you really are! Half an hour ago I felt like death, and now I'm laughing fit to bust my ribs!"

"You're glad I came, then Miss?" His face was gentle and appealing, a look she had never seen before, and her laughter was instantly dispelled by the growing happiness within her.

She looked at him for a long, thoughtful

moment, recognising in his hopeful expression and pleading eyes the same needs as she herself had, but which she had never truly acknowledged until now.

She and Manny both needed to be wanted — to be loved. It was as simple as that. She smiled, watching his smile answer hers. So strange that she should feel like this about a child, when she had never liked them before. Strange that two children had suddenly entered her life as a result of the frustrating Sennerton visit: Manny and Sarah.

Sarah . . .

An amazingly simple solution to the problem of what to do with Manny suddenly hit her. The boy could stay for a day until the weekend, and on Friday evening after work she would drive him home to Sennerton, in time for Sarah's birthday party on Saturday.

She-flew to the phone. "Let's send that telegram. I'll write it down first — er — what was it? 'Mission accomplished. Safe and well, Home Friday p.m. Don't worry. Love, Manny.'"

Manny hurled himself into the most comfortable armchair while she read the telegram over the phone. Then, as she returned to sit opposite him, he said matter of factly. "Not as good as mine was, but I reckon it'll do. Now what shall we do next? Tell your fortune, shall I? Get the cards out then, Miss. My golly, I aren't half looking forward to seeing that ole Bloody Tower . . . "

Later on she tucked him into the spare bed and left the door ajar, returning to the sudden emptiness of the lounge. What an extraordinary day it had been! She was tired but somehow uplifted. Tomorrow she would wangle a few hours off work and take Manny sight-seeing, and then on Friday they would drive down to Sennerton together. A night at the Black Dog once again, and then Sarah's birthday party —

She smiled as she went into her own bedroom, admitting to herself that it would be lovely to be back in Sennerton — yes, even after all the problems she had encountered there. Lovely, especially, to see Sarah's welcoming smile.

Then her face grew serious. Was she, after all, wise to return? For a long time Robin sat before her dressing table, brushing her hair and thinking deeply, the old familiar conflicts returning stronger than ever.

Clearly, the village had no time for her, but Sarah did. And she couldn't disappoint Manny again . . . She looked at the wide, anxious eyes staring back from the mirror and knew, with a numbing certainty, that Sennerton — or could it be Britannia? — had indeed laid a spell on her. She had to go back. Had to visit Sentry House and feel its magnetic pull on her heart strings.

She smiled wryly as Guy's words flew into her mind, and then the smile died. What would it be like to see Tom again? Even more important, how would *he* feel on seeing *her*?

The morning was noisy and busy, and by the time Robin had spent a couple of hours at her desk while Manny fed the pigeons in Trafalgar Square, she felt quite worn out.

With Derek away a lot of extra responsibility fell on her shoulders, and the half-humorous note he had left on her desk rankled sourly . . . 'Gone to clear up your mess. Try not to get into any more trouble while I'm away. D.'

She sifted through a large pile of accumulated letters with the help of one of the girls from the typing pool, and then tackled the phone messages that needed action. At just after eleven forty-five she sighed with relief as the last note was tossed into the 'out' tray.

"Thank goodness, that's the lot." She smiled at Cleo, still scribbling hard, and pushed back her chair. "I'm going now, having an early lunch and then taking the afternoon off. Everything's up-to-date now and Miss Field will keep an eye open for the rest of the day. Friday's not usually very busy, is it . . . "

Cleo bit her pencil nervously. "Sorry, Miss Ford, but I've just remembered — there was a call for you yesterday, a personal one . . . "

Robin turned at the door. "When? And why didn't you tell me before? Who was it?" Her tone was sharp and the girl's cheeks coloured; she was fairly new to the pressures of the business world.

"Er — a Mr Devenish. He phoned late in the afternoon, just as I was leaving. Wouldn't leave a message when I told him you weren't here. I'm sorry, I should have said . . . "

"Never mind." Robin thought longingly that a warm word from Guy would have been more than welcome yesterday, but she knew it was no good sentimentalising things. It was unlikely that they would meet again, now that the Sentry House contract had been taken out of her hands. But she would have liked to have told him herself and said goodbye . . .

She left the office despondently, but by the time she had persuaded Manny to leave his new-found pets, and headed the Mini in the direction of the Tower, the usual optimism had returned. Manny's smile and his infectious good humour acted on her like a tonic; it really was fun, having the boy with her, and they spent a happy hour exploring the ancient building together.

"Cor!" he muttered, impressed to near-silence as he read the rough initials of centuries-old prisoners' names, carved on the dungeon walls. "Glad I don't have to stay here too long — dark, ain't it? An' cold. Let's get out, Miss . . . " Shivering, he raced up the uneven stone steps.

In the welcome crisp sunlight Robin walked him briskly back to the car. "That's it, then, Manny. In you get. We'll be on our way — with any luck, and not too much traffic, we'll be home in Sennerton by tea time."

"Home?" He gave her a sideways look, echoing the word, and she felt herself colouring. London was her home, always had been, so what was she talking about?

Manny twisted about beside her, keen eyes anxious to see everything as they drove along the crowded streets.

"Hey, stop, Miss! There's a shop there with a teapot in the window, it's got pictures of London on it. I gotta buy it for me Mum — a pressie from London, she'll be so chuffed she'll fergit to give me what fer fer running away!"

In the shop his hand fumbled in his pocket, and fished out five and a half pence. "Oh, lor . . . " The disappointment clouding his face hit her hard, so quickly she said, "Why, I quite forgot to reimburse you for your services, didn't I? What's the going rate in protection money, these days? Fifty p

112

an hour? That'll be — well, it'll cover the cost of that teapot, anyway! Come on, let's buy it."

While the gaudy teapot was being wrapped under Manny's eagle eye, Robin idly browsed among the crowded shelves. The pleasure on the boy's face had warmed her in a way she had never experienced before. Now she had started giving she didn't want to stop. Wasn't there someone else for whom she could buy a gift?

Of course — Sarah! Delighted, she searched for a suitable birthday present and soon found the very thing, a doll dressed as an old-fashioned Cockney flower girl, stiff arms carrying a basket and holding out a tiny nosegay. Instinctively, Robin knew Sarah would love it — the spirit of London itself a memory from the romance of days-gone-by.

Manny scoffed when he saw it. "Soppy thing, only a girl would want something like that! Now, a teapot's useful, but a doll . . . yuck!"

"Sometimes it's nice to have a present that isn't useful, Manny, something you can sit and look at and imagine all sorts of things about," said Robin mildly.

"Huh!" He got back into the car in disgust and then kept up a running commentary as they drove through the endless suburbs, finally emerging on the motorway and heading southwest for Devon.

When at last he stopped talking, the silence allowed her thoughts to concentrate freely on what lay ahead — her return to Sennerton, and the mixture of delights and anxieties that such a return held.

Firmly she told herself that she had every good reason to be going back — surely Sarah's birthday party was far more important than the possibility of any stupid village feeling against her. Why, she had almost forgotten the unpleasantness she had experienced there, both in the Black Dog, and on Tom Hewitt's doorstep. It wouldn't happen again, now that the sale of Sentry House was out of her hands. She was just a visitor, no longer involved in such things.

At this point, a gentle nodding pressure on her left shoulder showed her a sleeping

Manny; slowing down, she pulled into the first layby, gently supporting his head with a folded jacket, and pulling his gangling legs into a more comfortable position. Then, smiling to herself at the unlikelihood of Robin Ford, career-girl *par excellence* pandering to the whims and caprices of a wild gypsy boy, she drove on, steadily and optimistically, towards the small village that contained an old house which, as Guy Devenish had so rightly said, was tugging at her vulnerable heart strings.

7

IT was mid-afternoon by the time they left the motorway behind and drove deep into the Devon countryside, eventually reaching the familiar lanes just as the herd of brown cows plodded slowly into Sennerton.

"She's ready to calve," said Manny expertly, pointing out a huge-bellied, swaying beast, trailing wearily behind her sisters. "I s'pect old man Dunstan's got the vet in, she's a difficult one, she is."

"How do you know, Manny?" Robin was vastly impressed.

"I see what's going on, don't I? Farming's all birth and death anyway, see, Miss . . . hey, look there's Uncle Nip!" Manny twisted around like an eel, grinning back at the man walking briskly through the village.

In the mirror Robin caught a glimpse of Nip's heavy face: as he recognised his nephew's exuberant smile, a returning smile flashed out. She saw undoubted welcome and love, and clear relief that the run-away was safely home. Something touched her, deep inside; if only there was someone who felt like that about her.

Determinedly, she said, "We'll go straight to your home and I'll book a room at the pub afterwards." It was important to see Manny reunited with his family, even though she was slightly in awe of Charlie and Brit, with their direct, no-nonsense attitudes.

The summerhouse was full of lamplight and shadows and as soon as the Mini's wheels crunched to a halt on the gravel outside, Brit's stern face peered through the uncurtained window. Robin heard a shout as the door opened, and saw Manny leap out of the car, straight into his mother's arms.

"I'm back! I'm safe! Don't be cross, Mum . . . did you get the telegram? Did you keep it? Musta cost a bomb — what did Dad say?"

Charlie loomed through the darkness, big, overbearing and more than a little frightening. "Never mind what I said, it's what I'm saying *now* that matters. Where the hell you bin, you little varmint? I'll take my belt to you, so I will . . . "

Manny didn't seem too disturbed by his father's growling threats. He hugged his mother and thrust the parcel at her. "Here, open this! Quick! Cor, you never seen anything like this before — . Miss took me to the Bloody Tower, and we saw the ravens and the dungeons and . . . "

Brit's dark eyes stared accusingly over the top of his head. "You took him away from us, you did." Her voice was baleful and Robin's smile faded rapidly.

"No, Mrs Lee, I certainly didn't. He came on his own — I had no idea that — "

Suddenly Manny left his mother, flying back to Robin and standing protectively at her side. " 'Twasn't her fault! I wanted to go, that's all. Tore me off a strip, she did — but then she was O.K. and let me stay. Hey, Mum, you know what? I had a bath *indoors*!"

Robin held her breath and felt the sharp indecision that flashed from Brit's stony face to Charlie's beetle-browed face. She prayed they would believe their son; she had had enough unpleasantness lately in Sennerton — wouldn't it be nice if Brit and Charlie decided to be friendly? But how unlikely.

"Don't you go getting ideas above you, boy: a bath indoors, indeed. Well — " Brit hesitated briefly, exchanging a last glance with Charlie. Then she looked directly at Robin. "You'd like some tea, I daresay," she suggested baldly.

Robin relaxed and a warm glow ran through her. "I'd love a cup, Mrs Lee," she answered, smiling, and followed Brit into the summerhouse.

As she sat on the cluttered window-seat, watching Brit busy herself with an ornate tea service and the smoke-blackened kettle that bubbled on a spirit stove in the corner, Robin's thoughts returned to the only other place where she had felt the same warm, family atmosphere, and wondered, rather painfully, what Tom and Sarah would say when she called, later on, at Well Farm.

Charlie stood over her suddenly, face still dark with distrust. "What you come back 'ere for, then? Still on 'bout knocking the ole house down, eh?"

Robin refused to be intimidated any further and answered firmly, "I brought your son home, Mr Lee; and I'm going to Sarah Hewitt's birthday party tomorrow. That's why I'm here. I've got nothing more to do with Sentry House now."

He snorted and sat down abruptly, taking a huge mug of tea from Brit. Robin sipped from her beautiful china cup, and tactfully changed the subject.

"What a lovely tea service, Mrs Lee. Bone china is always such a treat to drink from."

Brit's face cracked into a reluctant smile. "On'y brings it out special, we do."

"Then I'm honoured. Thank you."

"Well, you bin good to the boy. Little devil he is . . . we got that there telegram early this morning."

"I'm gonna frame it!" Manny chortled with glee.

"Shut yer mouth," said his mother imperiously. "Now you're home you better go and help Nip get the fire wood in. Get on, then — "

Manny gulped his tea and left, with a last dazzling grin at Robin.

"More tea?" Brit held out a hand heavy with broad gold-rings.

"No, thanks. That was lovely — just what I needed. Well, I'd better be off now, Mrs Lee."

"What's the hurry? Here, gimme your cup, I'll read the leaves." Brit solemnly swished more tea around the cup and then emptied the dregs on the earthen floor. A pattern of tea leaves remained on the floral china. She stared hard.

"I sees a man. Big. Grey-haired. And another — and clouds. I don't like it, what I sees . . . trouble with two strong men, that's what it is." Gravely she returned the cup to its saucer and waited for her guest to depart.

Robin stood up. "I know just what you mean! Trouble — " She sighed and then smiled wryly. "Thanks again for the tea. Goodbye, Mrs Lee." Then she paused and looked at the heavy figure in the far corner. Mr Lee — "

"Huh!" said Charlie noncommittally, but Robin thought that while little she could see of him wasn't quite so fierce as it had been a few minutes ago.

She was climbing back into the Mini

121

when Brit's voice reached out. "Come again. Next time I'll do the cards, see."

Robin drove slowly up the drive, her mind full of surprising thoughts of Brit and Charlie and Manny. She had never even bothered to think about how gypsies lived before . . . now she longed to know more, and to be included in their family circle again.

She passed a grey shape standing beyond the railings, and heard Chatterbox's wail of anguish fill the wintry afternoon. A thought hit her, ugly and despairing. What would happen to the poor old moke if the Lees had to leave their summerhouse and the free pasture? Manny had said the animal was too old to go on the road again — who would give him a home? Or would he be despatched to the knacker?

The answer flew into her mind with a directness that startled her. Why couldn't Tom Hewitt have Chatterbox at Well Farm as a pet for Sarah? Robin was sure she had read somewhere that handicapped children often reacted well to ponies and donkeys — how marvellous if Sarah could be taught to ride! Then the dream faded as fast as it had come; did she dare to suggest such an idea to Tom? Realistically, she had to admit that she didn't. But the thought persisted until she reached the lights of the pub.

Ted Mullins met her in the hall as soon as she stepped inside, and she had the immediate impression that he had been watching and waiting for her. She thought he looked most uncomfortable.

"Evening, Ted. Is Mr Harman still here? I'm not sure how long he planned to stay, but I'd like a room too, please."

Avoiding her eyes, he turned away to straighten a picture on the wall. "He left this morning, Miss Ford."

"Oh, I see . . . " Robin guessed that Derek must have had a swift and successful meeting with Tom Hewitt last night; so all was solved, was it? Her satisfaction was marred by the niggling thought that it was so unfair that Derek should have solved the problem, while she had tried to hard and yet had not succeeded. Then Ted's next words sent the thought flying.

"Things were a bit awkward, like, last night, Miss Ford. Bit of a rumpus, there was. And Mr Harman decided not to stay any longer."

Her stomach seemed to be sinking. "What do you mean, a rumpus? A — a row?"

"That's it. Nip Lee and your Mr Harman nearly came to blows, they did, in the bar. And Tom Hewitt didn't exactly help . . ."

"Oh no!" Robin felt her spirits quail. So nothing had been resolved, after all. "Was it — I mean, did Mr Harman start the trouble with Mr Hewitt? Or was it Tom . . . ?"

She could just imagine: Derek, with his determination that Tom should give in, and Tom being equally bloody-minded, refusing to yield an inch. And then, to cap it all, Nip in his cups, joining in the argument! She shuddered. "How unpleasant, Ted. I'm sorry, for you, nothing worse than other people's rows."

He nodded, meeting her eyes at last, his pleasant face grave and unsmiling. "That's right, Miss Ford. Bad for business it is, too. And that's why I'm afraid I can't offer you a room again." He glanced down at her overnight bag and then back at her troubled face. "You see, Miss Ford, you're too difficult a customer for me . . . all this row that's building up about Sentry House, well, I just don't want to be involved. So you'll have to go. I'm sorry, but that's how it is."

A lengthy silence grew as they stared at each other, and Robin felt her quick anger rise after the initial sharp shock of surprise and anxiety. "But that's quite ridiculous! I have nothing at all to do with Sentry House any longer! Mr Harman is dealing with the matter now, not me. I've simply come down to the village to bring Manny Lee home and to go to Sarah Hewitt's birthday parry tomorrow . . . "

Ted lifted one eyebrow and grinned abruptly. "My word, you're a stayer, you are! Sarah's birthday, eh? With Tom still in one of his blinding rages? Rather you than me, if you don't mind me saying so! No, take my advice, Miss Ford, you'd be better off going back to London than staying in Sennerton just now, with the feeling like it is. I don't feel very happy about things at all. And your Mr Harman didn't exactly help things along, the way he behaved, you know . . . "

"I can just imagine." Damn Derek and his pig-headed ferocity. But then, that wretched Tom was just as bad; both as awkward as the other. Robin picked up her bag and marched briskly down the hall towards the door. "Goodnight, then, Ted. And thanks for the advice — which I have no intention of taking . . . "

The door swung to behind her and she was out in the cold darkness, angry, roomless, but defiant. No one was going to run her out of Sennerton! What an idea. She climbed back into the Mini and sat there, deliberating and fuming.

"I'll stay here, damn them all, even if I have to sleep in the car." Or she could drive into Exeter and book into the hotel where Guy was staying . . . it would be nice to see him again. Yes, perhaps that would be the best thing to do — and it would give her time to calm down before she called at Well Farm tomorrow morning. "Yes, that's what I'll do."

But she didn't. Something determined and steely inside her kept repeating that she wouldn't allow herself to be pushed around like this. The whole village seemed against her, and she was loth to give in a second time. Surely there was somewhere she could stay in Sennerton, instead of running away?

The answer came like a shaft of welcome light. Sentry House, of course! Rugs from the car, her overcoat, the flask of unfinished coffee and a couple of sandwiches she and Manny hadn't eaten on the drive down from London. She would be fine. Robin felt like cheering. Come what may, she intended to beat the village. If no one wanted her — and it was quite clear that they didn't, with the unlikely but possible exception of Britannia Lee — then she would be independent, and be damned to them all!

She drove off down the drive towards the house, black now against the engulfing clouds, and parked as close to the steps as she could, suddenly feeling a mite irresolute as the shadows lengthened on the ground and the trees beside the house groaned and bent in the whispering wind. Did she *really* want to get out of the car and step into the dark, empty shell of a house?

With a superhuman effort she did so whistling loudly in a brave attempt to mask her fear. A good thing she always kept a torch in the glove pocket. And she could remove the cushion of the passenger seat for a pillow . . . arms laden, and the torchlight wavering ahead of her, she crept up the broken steps and entered the gloomy, gaping hallway. The faint light explored the unseen menace of the invisible rooms beyond, and a stretch of curving balustrades ascending the stairs. Robin gulped and decided to bed down just where she was. She would rather die than go any further . . .

Something fluttered in a hidden corner, and her heart jumped. Bats? Rats, even? Panic threatened, but then her obstinate determination took over. She would stay here, come what may, and that was the end of the matter.

Two hours later she was huddled in the corner she had chosen, stiff and cold, with the coffee long ago drunk, and a rumbling pit in her stomach making demanding noises, dismayed at her own reactions to the silence and the darkness. When, earlier, she had decided to come here, she had had no idea just what it would be like, alone, in such a place. Could she possibly see the night through, after all?

"Perhaps it would be more sensible to go to Exeter . . . " She jumped as she heard her own voice, faint and indecisive, shatter the quietness that encompassed her. It sounded so weak and fearful that she was immediately ashamed of herself adding more firmly "Stupid! Of course I'll stay! Nothing to be afraid of nothing at all, and once I'm asleep I won't know how cold it is —"

Sleep, that was the thing. She rearranged the rug and the leather cushion and snuggled into her coat. Deep breathing, it said in all the magazines she'd ever read: counting sheep. Oh, if only she could relax.

She had just dropped off when something woke her, panic again immediately stabbing and numbing. What was it? A rustle? A step? Of course not — there was no one about, what a fool she was!

But there is was again. Definitely a crunch on the gravel outside, and coming nearer, up the steps . . . Robin's aghast mind filled with remembered stories of violence and horror, and, sitting up, she braced herself against the wall. If only she had a weapon. She picked up the torch, useless now as the battery had long ago given out, and grasped it in a trembling hand. At least she would give a good account of herself when the intruder was near enough —

"Robin? Are you there?" It was a blessedly familiar voice.

"Oh!" She leaped to her feet, panic turning magically to thankful relief. "Oh yes, yes, I'm here . . . " Stepping hastily into the darkness, she nearly fell over the rug at her feet, and kicked it away as she rushed towards the doorway. The circle of light from a powerful lamp advanced and she found herself face to face with the owner of the voice.

"Tom, I'm so glad to see you!" Her voice cracked and she reached out for him spontaneously, realising now just how terrified she had been.

The lamp dimmed as he put it down, and then strong arms were about her, folding her safe, gentle words quietly hushing her fears, reassuring her.

"What on earth are you doing here, you silly creature? Ted Mullins told me you'd been to the pub and that he'd decided not to give you a room — well, that was bad enough, and I told him exactly what I thought of him — but then he said he'd seen you drive up towards the old house ... so I came to see if he was right. I know the sort of girl you are, you see — determined, independent, pig-headed ... "

The insulting words sounded like compliments, with a hint of laughter attached to them. Robin stirred in Tom's arms and smiled through the darkness.

"I'm beginning to think I'm just an idiot myself really; oh Tom, thank you for coming. It's so spooky here, and so dark — and there's a bat, or an owl or something keeps swishing through the doorway. And those ghastly trees, groaning all the time."

She was able to laugh now as she stepped away from him. He loosened his arms and let her go, but she was conscious of his eyes following her. Gripping her self-control very firmly, she sat down on the car rug once more and patted a place beside her. "Do take a seat! Mind you, I'm not used to having company in my bedroom, but let's hope no one will ever know!"

He put the lamp halfway up the staircase so that the mellow light fell softly from a distance, leaving their faces in shadow. Then he sat down beside her, heaving a flask and a parcel out of his jacket pockets.

"Here you are, super-woman — supper. I had a feeling you'd be starving, if you were here. Janet's a dab hand at pasties, and I put a slug of brandy in the coffee."

Robin glanced at him humbly. "You mean, you went to all this trouble, just for me? And you weren't even sure that I was here — "

He grinned back sarcastically. "Don't worry yourself I was pretty certain you were. You're such a stubborn creature, I couldn't see you accepting defeat and leaving the village again, not without a fight. Here, eat your pastie."

"But — "

"Eat it. Plenty of time for talking later." He poured out a mug of steaming coffee and put it on the floor in front of her.

Robin thought she had never tasted anything so good as Janet's pastie, and revised her ideas of the housekeeper's true worth. When she'd finished eating, and was slowly sipping the laced coffee, she looked quizzically at Tom, sitting there so quietly, immersed in thought. "Now what?"

He turned to meet her eyes, and she felt an immediate return of the strange feeling that his direct gaze had evoked in her when first they met.

Here was a man who expected nothing but the truth from life, and from all whom he met. A difficult man, quite unlike anyone else she had ever met. A man you either hated or loved . . . catching her breath she sought desperately for words to ease the quick emotion that unexpectedly threatened to swamp her.

"Go on, then, say it! What you're thinking — that I've got a nerve coming back, after all you said to me. That I'm a nuisance — what did you call me? — a pest!" She sounded far braver than she felt, but kept her head high, flying

133

her smile like a flag of triumph, waiting tensely for him to answer.

Certainly she didn't expect him merely to smile back and say casually and quietly, "Mind if I smoke? I think better when the old pipe's going."

"Of course not. As long as you don't throw sparks around . . . and set the place on fire? That would just about solve the whole problem, wouldn't it? No more rumours of what's going to happen, no more personal rows between people — " He held her eyes, still smiling. Then his face grew serious. "But I didn't come here to talk about the house."

Bemused by the uncharacteristic gentleness of him, Robin said, foolishly, "So why did you come?"

"For an intelligent woman you say the silliest things sometimes. Isn't it obvious that I came to find you? To see if you were safe? You were very much on my mind, Robin, after that last outburst of mine . . . I couldn't seem to get rid of you, try as I did." His eyes were fiercely hypnotic in the dim light, his smile gone, and she felt herself weaken.

"That was — nice of you, Tom."

"Nice be damned! Sarah would never forgive me if I let her favourite birthday guest die of cold and fright!" The old mockery had returned in full force, and she blinked as she realised, yet again, that Tom was never the same person twice running.

Quick frustration, and a certain embarrassment at her own frailty, made her voice angry and loud. "You're impossible! You're like a damned chameleon, always changing colour! No wonder Derek Harman had a row with you last night — I don't blame him, you're certainly the most irritating man I've ever met!"

Their eyes clashed abruptly, but he didn't appear disturbed, which surprised and enraged her even more, merely took the pipe from his mouth and stared at it while she fumed and wondered what to do next. When he spoke, the words were quiet, yet the mockery made her squirm.

"Why are you so angry? Disappointed that I didn't make a pass at you? Oh no — I leave that sort of thing to more worldly customers; like our good friend Guy Devenish . . . I'm sure he's far more experienced in that line than I could ever be. Just a simple country boy, that's me. Sorry I didn't come up to your expectations, Robin . . . "

She had no witty and crushing retort; and while she sat there, gasping and searching for words, he changed moods yet again. Suddenly he stood up, grabbing her wrist and pulling her with him.

"I've got something to show you. Come on."

Protesting, she was drawn, willy-nilly, towards the stairs, where he picked up the lamp, paying no attention to her useless efforts to withdraw her hand from his. "Mind the steps. That's it — careful, now . . . "

They were outside on the gravel, the house a gigantic black blur beside them. Half-way down the drive lights glowed softly in the summerhouse and the nearby caravan, and murmurs of music wafted up from a transistor.

Robin gulped, her sense of humour returning. "This would be quite romantic, if it wasn't so damned silly; really, Tom, I do wish you'd go home and let me — "

"Shut up." The terse words made her angry again. He marched her along the path until they reached the neglected stable block, an elegant tower outlined against the vault of black above, and a clock with crazy, out-of-order hands, shining in the beam of the directed lamplight, as Tom slowly shone it around the huddle of stone buildings.

"When I was a boy I played here. I swung on the beams, pinched the swallows' eggs, teased the horses and drove the old man's groom mad. I loved every stick and stone of the place. I still do."

He turned quickly and stared down at her, the blaze of his gaze holding her silent and impressed. "Remember that, will you, when you're calling me names and accusing me of making trouble? I've got reasons for wanting to keep Sentry alive, better reasons than your friend Guy Devenish and smart boss Derek Harman can ever hope to think up when they're trying to fix a price on the place . . . "

He turned away, staring over the cobbled yard, his thoughts and memories clearly traversing the years.

Robin discovered she was deeply moved. Had she misjudged him, after all? He was such a strange man, full of moods and passions. But slowly she was beginning to learn that he had one constant character trait which over-rode all the others; he loved Sentry House, and would never change.

She knew now, with a depth of new respect, that Tom had far more to him than a blustering manner resulting often in a devil of a temper, a certain rural charm and devastating blue eyes. She laid a hand on his arm and he looked up, startled, as if he had forgotten she was there. "Thanks for telling me. I do understand, Tom."

"Do you?" His voice was bitter. "I wonder. A town girl, living such a different life? Have you ever felt as I do about a house — a place, even? Does your own home mean anything to you? I doubt it . . . " He looked down at her sombrely, and she thought, with a flash of self-pity, that he would be more understanding if he knew that she had no real home, except the small suburban flat just off the main road in Ealing, and that could hardly evoke such passion as he felt for Sentry House.

It took her a moment to control her face and her voice, but she succeeded, saying gently, "No, Tom, I've never felt so deeply about anywhere that I've lived; until I came here. And now — well, Sentry House has put a spell on me, too, I think."

The words seemed to come out on their own, and she was surprised to hear them; she hadn't intended to tell Tom how she felt . . .

"Do you mean that, Robin?"

She saw the bitterness on his face recede. "Yes, I do, Tom."

They stared at each other, close as never before, with truth forging a new bond between them. Then, slowly, his smile flashed out again. "Well, I'm glad. It makes everything different, somehow, doesn't it?"

A wild impulse to reach up and kiss him enveloped her. But instead she smiled and waited, knowing that Tom Hewitt was an old-fashioned man with old-fashioned attitudes, and must act in his own time. It was a nice, reassuring thought.

"Robin — " He came closer, but as he spoke, an ugly sound of raised voices in the distant broke the silence of the night. "What on earth — ?" She turned quickly, alarmed.

His face grew grim. "Sounds like Charlie Lee. More trouble at the pub, I expect. I'd better get back. Are you all right here? Take the lamp. I'll come back when I've sorted it out . . . "

He was on his way before she knew it, footsteps fading quickly as he ran down the drive.

Suddenly chilled and more alone than ever before, Robin pulled her coat closer around her trembling body and picked up the heavy lamp. Violence in the night — and all because of her.

Even though her reasoning powers reminded her that the conflict of the future of the old house actually lay in Guy's urge to sell, her emotions over-rode their logic. She had come here first and stirred things up; she had brought the pot to the boil. And now — what?

Decision hit her. She took a last

look at the stables where Tom had left his childish heart and hurried back to the car, knowing exactly where she was going, and what she must do.

For the sake of peace in Sennerton, she must drive to Exeter and persuade Guy to give up all idea of selling Sentry House.

8

THE WHITE STAG was welcoming and comfortable, and Robin heaved a sigh of relief as she entered. It was quite true what Tom had said, that she was fundamentally a town girl, used to having all the creature comforts, and therefore not really at home in the country. And yet she was learning fast to accept the disadvantages and appreciate the serenity of rural life; she told herself she would argue the point out with him the next time they met, for she did feel a most insistent, increasing affection for haunted old Sentry House.

"Mr Devenish?" The night porter answered her query and led her down the elegant foyer. "In the cocktail lounge, Madam. This way, please."

The tall, dark-suited figure with the prematurely greying hair rose from the stool where he sat at the end of the curving bar and stared at her with surprise as she approached.

"Robin! What a nice surprise! It's good to see you again — "

"Thanks, Guy. I'm sorry to come so late, but I badly need to talk to you."

"Right. But let me get you a drink first."

She was impressed and more than a little flattered that he remembered her liking for a dry martini without being reminded. He stared curiously as they settled themselves in a quiet corner. "Anything wrong? You look a little — "

"Dishevelled?" She put a hand to her windblown hair and smiled wryly. "I'm not surprised! I've been camping out in Sentry House because that wretched Ted Mullins at the Black Dog wouldn't let me have a room for the night."

Guy got up immediately, frowning. "Is that so? Well, I'll have a sharp word with Mr Mullins in the morning. But in the meantime, I'm going to book you a room here, right away. Now just sit there and relax, I'll be back directly."

Robin did as he said, feeling cosily soothed and cossetted by the affluence and comfort of the hotel, her battered ego uplifted by Guy's masterful manner.

How lovely it was to have a personable man looking after her.

Then she remembered Tom bringing the pastie and coffee and felt something of a traitor, for he, too, had been looking after her in his own manner. If only she didn't have to keep comparing them . . .

Guy returned and pulled his chair a fraction nearer. "Your room's all organised and I've ordered soup and an omelette as you probably haven't eaten properly — no, don't argue, let me know what's best. Now what's all this about then, Robin?"

Abruptly tongue-tied, she sought to find the right words to convince him of the growing conflict in Sennerton. It was vital that she gave him a graphic picture of the way things were going before coming to the crux of the matter and asking him to change his mind about selling Sentry House.

She sipped her drink and cautiously looked at him over the rim of the glass. Tall, handsome, magnetic; yes he was certainly attractive. And she knew he found her attractive, too. In a way, what she was about to do was a form of emotional blackmail — do as I ask *because you're already a little in love with me* . . .

It wasn't a nice thought. For a second she wavered, but then the memory of Tom showing her the old, beloved stables, and the expression on his intent face as he remembered his boyhood, supplanted her own personal feelings. For the sake of the whole village, she must be honest with Guy.

She met his eyes then and recognised the cool, assessing stare of a true businessman, beneath the masking, patient smile. That gave her courage, for Guy Devenish wasn't a lover — not yet; she was merely talking business, and she would do well to remember the fact.

Suddenly it was easy to begin. "Guy, the reason Ted Mullins wouldn't let me have a room tonight was because of the feeling in the village over the proposed sale of Sentry House . . . he said I was too hot to handle — oh, not in so many words! But that was what he meant. Bad for his business. Someone who would provoke conflict . . . do you remember when we first spoke over the phone, you hinted that Sennerton might not like the idea of the house being redeveloped as a holiday complex?"

He nodded, narrowing his eyes slightly.

Robin felt a reassuring growth of confidence and went on. "Well, you were right. And things have now got to the point when conflicting attitudes are out in the open with a vengeance; I'm afraid they could even result in real violence. Already there have been several arguments at the pub, and this evening there was actually a fight — "

He leaned back, shoulders squared under the elegant navy barathea jacket, finishing his drink, never taking his eyes off her face. "I'm sorry to hear it Robin, but not surprised. My friends in the village hinted that the population was divided in its loyalties and that feelings ran high."

She paused. His face was like a rock, displaying no emotion at all. Did he guess what she was leading up to? Hurriedly she went on.

"I knew you would be sorry. After all, even if you never actually lived in the village, your family did, and so you

146

must have some idea of the enormous influence Sentry House had had, for years, on the villagers — for centuries, even."

He shifted in his chair, and she saw the steely grey eyes narrow imperceptibly in a look of quick irritation. "What exactly have you come here for, Robin? Hardly to give me a blow by blow account of petty squabbles between prejudiced peasants, I think. I know you're a competent and utterly professional business woman and as such I respect your judgement; so don't beat about the bush any longer. Let's get down to the core of things; just why are you here?"

Even now it would be easy to fool him, she thought unhappily — she had only to smile, veil her eyes coquettishly, say she needed company after the unpleasantness of Sennerton; only had to murmur, "I knew you were still here, Guy; why don't we leave the business for another day?" Perhaps yesterday she might have done just that, but now the inner convictions were much stronger. It would be false and wrong to deny them.

She took a deep breath and looked

straight into his deep-set eyes. "I'm asking you to stop the sale, Guy. That's what I've come for."

"Exactly what I thought." He drained his glass and leaned over the table until his face was very close to hers, his words quiet and full of impact. "You see, I'm beginning to get to know you better, Robin — like I said the other evening, you're warm-hearted and concerned about other people; so much so that the idea of the village being split in half over Sentry House's proposed, redevelopment has warped your business sense." His mouth lifted into a half-smile and instantly Robin was up in arms. How dare he patronise her!

"You're saying I'm behaving like an hysterical woman! Well, I assure you that's not true — "

He cut her short abruptly, eyes ice-cold. "That's not at all what I said. Don't put words into my mouth."

So it was to be war! She sat up straighter and stared defiantly at him. "Guy, please forget I'm a woman and — "

Unexpectedly, the ice thawed, and he

148

grinned appreciatively. "Rather hard to do that, my dear!"

She ignored the interruption. "First and foremost, I'm interested in my firm's offer, of course. And even though Derek Harman, my boss, has taken over the handling of the job, I'm still involved, whether I like it or not. Believe me, Guy, emotion simply doesn't enter into the fact that I can see the village being shattered by such a sale. Observation is enough. And no one can condone violence, surely? Doesn't your own family background make you feel you must do something to stop such a situation arising?"

Breathless, but pleased with her eloquence, she leaned back and took another sip of her drink. She had put the fact in a nutshell — how would he get out of that?

Guy replaced his empty glass on the table and smiled broadly at her, an admiring smile that made him appear anything but the relentless tycoon and completely took the wind out of her sails. What was he playing at now?

"Honestly, Robin, you're far too good

for your down-to-earth employer! A girl with your potential should be acting as peace emissary at international conferences! I can see you thawing the heart of the coldest and most prejudiced diplomat — ah, here's your supper."

She stared disconsolately at the steaming soup, and then back at him. "I'm waiting for your answer, Guy. Never mind the compliments — exactly what are you going to do about the problem?"

The smile died and the ruthless coldness, which she guessed had only been momentarily banished, flashed out again. "I'm going to do just what I always intended to do, Robin — which is to sell Sentry House to Harman if he offers me the right price."

His words were like stones plummeting down into her dismayed mind. She had known all along that he was relentless, and yet there had been moments of such warm and kindly perception between them that she had hoped — stupidly, perhaps — that if she pleaded hard enough he would give in. Now she stirred the soup thoughtfully, trying to hide the disappointment that racked her, determined still to find his Achilles heel.

Desperately she thought of Sentry House and its elegant facade. Surely there must be some way of preserving the beautiful old building? Hope stung briefly, and she looked up at him impulsively. "One last word, Guy — I accept that you mean to sell Sentry, come what may, but wouldn't you consider finding another buyer, someone who wouldn't be as drastic with the property as Derek intends to be? Someone, perhaps, who would be content merely to restore it, use it as a hotel, say, or a nursing home? If only it could stay as it is, the village would be satisfied, I'm sure."

Quietly and with great finality, Guy said, "The only thing that might influence my decision would be to get a better proposition than the one I've already had from Harman. And I can't foresee any crack-brained little enterprise being able to do that. No, Robin, you're wasting your time and your energy, my dear. Now, eat your supper before it gets cold."

It was obvious that the matter was ended; obediently she did as he said, but the food was now tasteless and unappetising as she mulled over his last words. She acknowledged his honesty, but found the ruthlessness of it difficult to accept.

At last she pushed aside her plate and said numbly, "I'm sorry, but I can't manage any more. I think perhaps I'll go to my room." She looked at him, trying to clear her churning mind of her intense disappointment. "You've been very good to me, Guy — I'm sorry it's turned out like this. Now, if you'll excuse me — "

He was at her side as she arose, a solicitous hand beneath her elbow, that magnetic smile lifting his face into a caring, understanding smile. "I know you're tired; but why don't we just have a breath of air before you turn in? It's so stuffy in here. Come on — just a stroll along the Close . . . "

It was impossible to deny him, and why should she? Wearily, Robin felt she had no will of her own left. Perhaps, as he said, the night air would revive her flagging spirits. "All right, then — just a few minutes."

A church clock was chiming ten thirty

as they strolled across the cobbled yard and looked at the moon shining on the smooth lawns surrounding the Cathedral. The stonework on the ancient building learned and shone in the eerie light as it shafted down from between fast-scudding clouds, and Robin caught her breath in delight.

"It's so beautiful — so very old — what is it about places like this, I wonder, that makes one want to look after them, to keep them in good repair — to love them almost?"

"A sense of history, I guess. Something you obviously possess and I don't. I'm sorry we don't see eye-to-eye about certain matters, Robin, but I hope it won't change the fact that we have shared feelings about other things . . . for instance, the romance of this particular moment. Moonlight, you, me, and a need to share our emotions. Don't tell me you don't feel it too . . . " They paused under the shadowy canopy of a huge tree and he gently pulled her into his arms.

The moment was suddenly charged with something she could not withstand. Thickly, she murmured, "Yes — no

— oh Guy . . . " and then she was close to him, swept up into the passion of his embrace. His lips were on hers, gentle, then strong and urgent, and it was as if they became one channel of longing and feeling.

When they drew apart, she was breathless and starry-eyed, full of wonder at what had happened. Guy laughed gently at her radiant face, and ran a finger down her cheek.

"You're marvellous! I've never met anyone quite like you before — and for me that's quite a confession. Come on, time we went back. Bed for you and a last nightcap for me. And then there's tomorrow to think about but we'll let that look after itself for the moment. Let's say goodnight again, Robin, my sweet . . . "

Strolling slowly back to the hotel, his arm about her waist, at last Robin came down to earth and knew, numbly that, despite her happiness, the problem still wasn't in any way solved. Nothing had happened to change how she felt about Sennerton, even though she knew she felt differently about Guy after that last tremendous kiss.

As they approached the door of the hotel, she said impulsively, "You'll hate me for saying this, but I'm still going to do everything I possibly can to save poor Sentry House; oh, Guy, surely — if you're fond of me, and I think you are . . . " Catching her breath, she was suddenly afraid, but still determined. " . . . surely you'll think twice about your decision, and do as I ask? *Please* don't sell Sentry House to Derek — for my sake, Guy — ?"

In the doorway she stared at him, abruptly regretting bitterly what she had just said. Had she killed that precious moment they had shared out there, in the shadow of the old Cathedral? Was her bargaining too much for him to accept?

And then another terrible thought stabbed her; was she selling herself?

Guy's eyes raked her face, his hands strong and warm about hers. Then, slowly, he said, "Have you quite forgotten what I said? That only a *better proposition*" — he underlined the words meaningfully — "would make me change my mind? Well, can you think of one? I can. Perhaps a proposition between the two of us, rather than between me and your Mr Harman. You see, it's completely up to you, Robin — "

Shattered, as the explicit intent of his words reached her, she slid her hands out of his grasp, her face falling and a chill tingle running through her body. Yes, she did understand; and only too well. She had been right; she *was* selling herself and he was prepared to buy . . .

So Guy would willingly trade Sentry House for her love. It was as simple as that. Could she do it? Confusion filled her, and hurriedly she turned away, so that he shouldn't see her bewildered expression. In the foyer she headed for the stairs, turning only at the last moment to meet his questioning eyes.

"I need time, Guy, to think this over," she said in a low, uneven voice. "Let me go to bed now, it's been quite a day, one way and another."

"Of course. I understand. We'll talk about it tomorrow. Sleep well, my love." There was a tenderness in his words, and the warmth of his expression made tears burn her eyelids. She went up the stairs feeling hopelessly lost. If only she could hate him! But there was too much in Guy Devenish, despite his dominating attitudes, that she found appealing and attractive — what on earth was she to do?

The clock in the Cathedral Close awoke her very early next morning, and at once her mind was swamped with the terrible predicament that surrounded her. But at least the feeble sunshine filtering in through the uncurtained window of her room brought with it a certain fresh optimism and hope — life still went on, she told herself and a new day awaited her. She was by nature a fighter; she would find a solution, come what may.

After an early, solitary breakfast, she wrote a hasty note to Guy, promising to be back in time for dinner. "Bear with me," she scribbled, "I'll give you your answer then."

It was with a guilty feeling of having shelved a very difficult issue, though, that she left Exeter, heading back to the remoteness of Sennerton. But, even as she brooded dismally, the glory of the morning's frosty freshness, and the gentle, changing colours of the stretching landscape, brought a new feeling of serenity.

She was suddenly charged with increasing strength and knew that somehow, during the day, she would come to a decision and know just what to say to Guy, later in the evening.

9

THE village seemed to welcome her as she entered it. The farm dog's high-pitched bark, as it heard the Mini stop beside the green, was familiar and pleasant, so was the creaking sign outside the Black Dog, noisy in the sharpening wind. Robin got out and looked about her with a feeling of nostalgia; it was as if she had come home.

Briskly she headed for Sentry House. On a lovely crisp morning like this a walk would be just the thing — maybe she would see Manny, too. The rhythm of walking, the growing warmth of the sun, and the beauty all around her proved the perfect panacea to last night's upset, and she loitered first by the stream and then again at the old stable block, soothed by all she heard and saw.

Then, boldly, she entered the house itself and explored the silent rooms, noticing things she had missed before;

159

in particular an initial scratched on one of the small leaded panes of glass in the huge front room — who had PD been, and why was it so important to note the date, 1761? Robin's busy mind wove possible reasons for the engraving, and so she didn't notice the lithe shadow that paused at the doorway behind her.

Manny roared delightedly as she turned, startled. "Gotcha! Scared you, eh?"

Her heart swelled a little. "Of course not! Oh, I am glad to see you — but why aren't you at school; what's the reason this time, you wicked little truant?"

He patrolled the echoing room, peering curiously around him. "Too much to do for that ole school business. I gotta help with the party, see? Get the chairs and tables out, shove the pianner around . . . it's going to be a proper do, I can tell you. I sneaked into the kitchen when they weren't looking just now, and cor, the things they're cooking!"

His brilliant eyes gleamed and Robin laughed. Never before had she realised that a child could communicate such happiness and fun. "Sausage rolls?" she suggested, amused.

"You bet! And little 'uns on sticks, an' great bits of ham and stuff — I'll be there early, see if I'm not."

"All spruced up and clean?"

His face fell. "You would have to go and spoil things, wouldn't you — "

Robin took pity on him. "Sorry. You're lovely as you are. Manny, can you spare a few minutes before you disappear again? I'm at a loose end — I'd enjoy another walk around the grounds . . . "

"O.K." He was out of the door before she knew it, his urgent voice calling from the hall as he headed for the drive. "C'mon then — don't let's hang about. We'll go and get a cuppa tea from ole Ma Hannaman — hurry up, Miss!"

Mrs Hannaman's cottage was half-hidden in the fringe of ancient oak trees at the far end of Sentry grounds.

"Her ole man were a game-keeper; used to have a line o' dead crows and weasels and things hanging up, to scare the others off. I found some bones last time I came . . . " said Manny ghoulishly, pausing at the little garden gate.

Robin shuddered, and then said,

dubiously, "Ought we to go in? I don't know her — "

But already the front door was opening, and Mrs Hannaman's lined face beamed out a welcome. "Manny! Come in, boy — I've just put the kettle on. And who's your friend? Oh yes, bring her in, do — "

Mrs Hannaman was small and energetic, brimming with vivacity and interest. Robin stared discreetly around the tiny, over-crowded parlour with its mahogany and colourful bric-a-brac, while Manny gossiped in the kitchen. Tea arrived in blue willow-pattern cups and they all sat down and munched home-made biscuits.

"Well, I've heard about you, Miss Ford," said Mrs Hannaman forthrightly, and Robin waited uneasily for the verdict. "You've got a difficult job, that's for sure. I don't envy you." Her bright eyes twinkled suddenly. "But I don't blame you, neither, not like some I could mention!" Self-righteously, she folded small workworn hands over her nylon overall, and nodded with tightly compressed lips. "But haven't I seen you before, somewhere? There's a look on your face of someone familiar . . . "

As brisk as a lively squirrel, she jumped up and went to the sideboard, picking up a large framed photograph. "There!" Smiling triumphantly, she pointed out to Robin a blurred figure standing in a line-up of men and women in out-of-date dress, outside a large door. "Got her nose you have, and the way your hair grows . . . "

"Let's see." Manny peered over her shoulder. "Nab! That's nothing like Miss! Funny dresses, aren't they? Where did that photo come from then, Ma?"

Mrs Hannaman stared nostalgically at the old print, as she sat down again. "Taken at an outing of some sort, when my mother was working at Sentry in the old days. Oh, a long time ago now."

Robin kept silent, but her thoughts jostled busily. The face in the indistinct photo *did* resemble her a little — but she had never had any contact with Sennerton, nor, from what she knew of her parents' background, had they. And yet she felt so much at home here

— what could it all mean?

Drinking her tea, she listened to the racy comments on the forthcoming party that Manny tossed at Mrs Hannaman. At last he sprang to his feet restlessly, "C'mon! I gotta get back and help — thanks for the tea, Ma. See you again soon. Cheerio — "

Robin scarcely had time to thank Mrs Hannaman for her hospitality, but she knew she would remember the way her hostess looked at her as they left. "Yes, it's the nose. And the hair. Well, g'bye, my dear. Come again, won't you?"

As the church clock struck one Robin looked at Manny expectantly. "Off you go, your Mum will have dinner ready."

"Course she won't. Me Dad's out dealing and Mum don't bother till he comes home later. I usually get a bag of crisps . . . "

Robin took the hint obediently. "What a good idea. Be a love and go and get one for me as well, will you — here's some money." Manny raced towards the Black Dog with wings on his heels.

"Fried onion?" he shouted back over his shoulder, and she nodded, laughing to herself at his rapturous expression.

They ate sitting on a fallen beech log not far from Sentry House and then once again Manny was up and away. "Gotta help at the hall — see you later, Miss," and he was gone.

Robin sauntered back to the car to tidy herself as best she could. Then, with Sarah's brightly wrapped present in her hand, she went along to the village hall, on the far side of the church. She was early, but it would be interesting to see what was happening. Perhaps she might even be allowed to help with the preparations. But her optimism was immediately ground to ashes as the first face she encountered grew outraged and frosty.

The woman, youngish and hard-faced, scowled as she appeared, yelling over her shoulder, "Well, look who's here! The trouble-maker herself!"

Other heads peered out from the kitchen and Robin stood still, disconcerted by her reception. The young woman came a step nearer, laughing in Robin's face. "You've got a bloomin' nerve coming here! If I was you I'd get out, quick.

Your name's mud in the village, I can tell you. Nobody wants you here."

Robin flushed angrily, immediately determined not to let this unexpected attack defeat her. She gripped her self-control hard and made herself smile. "I'm sorry you think that," she said in a level voice. "I've been invited here by Sarah Hewitt, for her party; and I was wondering if I could do anything at all to help?"

Her adversary stared, quickly deflated. "Oh! Invited, were you? Well, I s'pose that makes a difference." She turned grudgingly back to the kitchen. "Here, May! Can she do anything to help?"

"Miss Ford, isn't it? I'm May Caunter." A smiling, elderly woman with astute eyes stepped forward, pointing briskly at the rows of hooks behind the entrance door, laden with coats. "Leave your jacket there and I'll find you an apron. The urn's not working again, so we've had to get all the old kettles out of the cupboard — they could do with a good scrub, if you really want something to do — "

Suddenly, Robin found herself in front

of a sink full of steaming water, grappling with an enormous old kettle which was all that Miss Caunter had said of it. As she worked and listened to the merry voices around her, she relaxed a little. The other women were shy of her at first, not sure whether to side with the first loud-mouthed attacker, or to follow May Caunter's example. But as excitement grew and the guests began to arrive, they forgot that Robin was a stranger in their midst, and started automatically including her in their chatter.

"Cold day, isn't it? Still, it's warm in here with the fires on — hope the little maid has a good party, she's such a dear child."

Robin discovered that she was enjoying herself, and when applause and shouts greeted Sarah's arrival, she clapped and cheered as loudly as everyone else.

Tom wheeled Sarah into the hall and Robin's heart beat quicker. What a handsome pair they were, all smiles, blue eyes fiercely happy as they greeted their numerous friends and well-wishers. She kept in the background, until Sarah's eager glance fell on her.

"Robin! Oh, I'm so glad you've come! Dad said you wouldn't be here . . . " Sarah gripped Robin's hand impulsively and put up her face to be kissed.

Bending towards the child's rosy cheeks, Robin felt Tom's eyes on her, and her pulses began to race. "Happy birthday, Sarah! Here's a little present," she said unsteadily; then Tom's voice chipped in, friendly and warm, "Good to see you, Robin," as he pushed Sarah's chair to the far end of the hall, where the top table was a sight for sore eyes, piled high with food and crowned with a scattering of colourful crackers and a huge iced cake.

Robin returned to the kitchen, bemused by the occasion and her own unexpectedly strong feelings. Thank goodness she could stay out of sight — it would be too much to have to face Tom now, feeling as she did. Last night she had been emotionally stirred by Guy's embrace, but now it was the mere sound of Tom's quiet, countrified voice that made her tense and brought the colour to her cheeks. Anyone would think she was a susceptible teenager, certainly not a grown career-girl, with a mind of her own. What, in heaven's name, was happening to her?

But the urgent demands for more tea, more sandwiches, more fruit drinks, soon made her forget her dilemma. The party was in full swing, music playing loudly from a record-player, and children's happy voices echoing around the hall. Suddenly, when the kitchen was empty and the crowd of helpers — Robin included — were gathered around the doorway, watching the fun, she felt a touch on her arm. Tom was at her side. His urgent expression made her catch her breath.

"I want to talk to you."

Willingly she followed him out of the hot hall into the faint sunlight of the cold late afternoon, not caring if suspicious eyes were watching. Tom wanted her; it was enough.

"I suppose you drove off to Exeter last night — to an hotel?" His words were carefully chosen and she knew instinctively that he had doubts about whether she had gone to find a comfortable bed or merely to seek out Guy; but he was too much of a gentleman to voice them.

She nodded, smiling back at him persuasively. "I — I needed a good night's sleep after those frightful two hours in the dark . . . " Better to leave it at that — she was in enough trouble as it was.

His watchful eyes flickered as if acknowledging her diplomacy.

"That was sensible. You did right to leave the village. I came to look for you later on, but you'd gone."

She nodded. "What happened at the pub?"

"A proper showdown." Tom looked grim and fierce, and her heart sank.

"More violence? Oh, Tom, how dreadful — was anyone hurt?"

"No. But it wasn't ended, I'm afraid. A couple of young louts from the new housing estate were in roaring form, and they won't let it rest there, I'm sure of it . . . but never mind that now. Are you enjoying the party? You should be in the hall, not hidden away out in the kitchen. Sarah asked me to find you and bring you in." Smiling, he reached out and took her hand. "Come on — we'll face the enemy together!"

Robin felt a pang of happiness stab through her, but wisdom made her shake her head. "It would be so easy for trouble to start again, and I'd do anything to avoid that, Tom."

His smile died. "I know that; which is more than I knew in the beginning. You see, I'm getting to understand you a bit better now, Robin . . . "

Tongue-tied, she stared back at him, the joy of the moment abruptly spoiled by the memory of Guy saying the same words last night. Then Brit's harsh voice echoed forebodingly around her mind — *two strong men: trouble.* She stepped away from him, suddenly aware of the truth of the gypsy's warning. Trouble indeed, and not just in the village itself but in her own personal life. Which man did she care for? If only she knew . . .

Then there was a roar of a motorbike engine revving up, and an appalling squeal of brakes. Voices rose in ugly clamour and Tom turned smartly around, his face set and angry. "Those young hooligans again! The ones who were on to me last night . . . if they come here, spoiling Sarah's birthday party, I'll — I'll — "

"Tom, come back!" But Robin's words were of no avail. He went purposefully down the road towards the little huddle of gleaming machines and black leather-clad youngsters, parked beside the village green.

Undecided, she dithered for a long, agonising moment. Should she fetch help? But that would interrupt the party, and Tom would never forgive her if she did that. Impulsively, she ran after him, not knowing what she could do to help, only painfully aware that he was in possible danger and that she must be there with him.

A nasty scene greeted her. Tom was shouting at a tall youth with straggling fair hair beneath his crash-helmet. She saw fists go up and the boy aimed a blow that missed. Tom retaliated and the lad's hand flew to his mouth, where blood flowed.

"I'll get you for that, Mr Bloody Know-it-all Hewitt! Or one of me mates will — "

In immediate response, a bike revved into action behind him, leading forward directly at Tom's uncompromising figure.

"Look out!" Robin's scream made him turn sharply, jumping out of the way of the approaching machine with only seconds to spare. With roaring exhausts and shouts of belligerent delight, the little gang drove off, hurtling up the road and out of sight.

But Tom hadn't been quite quick enough; he staggered to the roadside, left leg buckling under him. Robin flew to his side. "You're hurt!"

He collapsed, lying there in the gutter, pale suddenly beneath the weather-beaten skin, brilliant blue eyes grey with pain, and a moan escaping from his tight lips.

Inside Robin, a moment of terrible truth registered itself as she knelt beside him, her distraught eyes searching the ashen face. Would she have felt this way if it had been Guy Devenish lying there with blood on him, and pain making him look small and shrivelled? Suddenly, Guy became quite unimportant; all that mattered was that Tom should not be badly hurt.

"Tom — ," she choked. "Oh, Tom — I can't bear it, what can I do? Tom, please say something . . . "

But his eyes remained closed and the long agonising moment seemed to drag on for ever.

10

AT last the terrible moment ended. Tom slowly opened his eyes, moved his leg tentatively and grimaced. "It's all right — I think. Nothing broken after all. Help me up, will you, Robin — "

His face was still grey with pain and he grasped her arm until she winced beneath the pressure, as he stiffly got to his feet.

"Tom, let me go for help . . . "

"No." The one word was sharp and uncompromising. "I've got to get home. Sarah mustn't know about this." Gritting his teeth, he leaned heavily on Robin's shoulder and limped the short distance along the road to Well Farm.

The warm kitchen was deserted, save for a sleeping cat. Robin led him to the fireside chair, then found hot water and a towel.

Too lightly to mean it, Tom said, "Hardly a scratch! But it hurt like hell because that's the leg I broke a couple of years ago, when the tractor turned over on top of me in Stony Field — it's never been really right since. And that young thug landed me one in the same place, blast his eyes . . . "

Robin bathed the swollen, bruised leg and felt herself full of churning emotions. For one terrible moment she had thought him dead: things were happening so fast now that she could almost imagine she was on a see-saw — an unbalanced sensation, to say the least of it.

She tried to behave as casually as she knew he would wish. "You're lucky it didn't break again; look, you can see the imprint of the tyre under that bruise . . . oh, Tom, those dreadful boys! Where will all this end?"

Tom looked obstinate and tight-lipped. "If you uphold a cause you believe in, then you've got to be prepared to take some knocks from life," he said defiantly. Then his eyes met her and impulsively he reached out, touching her hand. "But I don't have to tell you that, do I? I've knocked you enough in the past few days. Robin, it's difficult for me to say

I'm sorry, but — well, I'm sorry . . . "

She wanted to laugh and weep at the same time, but managed somehow merely to smile back at his tense face, rising from her knees beside him and taking the bowl of water to the sink.

"Thanks, Tom," she said, trying hard to be matter-of-fact. "Now perhaps we really can be friends, after such a handsome apology!" She was grateful that he couldn't sense the tears pricking behind her eyelids.

Footsteps on the cobbled yard heralded Janet's arrival, wheeling Sarah home. "Oh, *you're* here . . . " Even the housekeeper's cold, insolent tone couldn't stop Robin's sense of abrupt happiness as she smiled back at Sarah's entranced face.

"Wasn't it lovely?" asked Sarah ecstatically, as Janet helped her out of the chair and onto the sagging couch beneath the window. The tabby cat stirred, arched its back, and then rearranged itself cosily in Sarah's small laps.

"Yes, it *was* lovely," answered Robin, going over and sitting beside the child. "And you were the belle of the ball, look at you, so pretty in that super dress!"

Sarah leaned back and yawned, suddenly weary. "Did you have parties like that when you were a girl?" Her curious eyes brought a pang to Robin's heart, and she said slowly, "No, no parties. I lived with my aunt and her family, and we were very poor. So we didn't have parties."

"What a shame. What about your mother and father? Did they live with your auntie, too?"

Robin felt Tom's intent eyes on her. She hesitated, remembered the loneliness of that bleak childhood returning to fill her with bitterness. When she answered her words were directed at Tom, although she looked at Sarah. "I didn't know my father. And my mother died when I was very little, so I didn't ever have a real family of my own, you see."

She didn't say that her mother had been unmarried and therefore the black sheep of her highly conventional relatives; she didn't speak of the vulnerable, childish years spent in constant, urgent longing for someone to love her as an individual, and not just as one of a hungry brood always clamouring for food and clothing. But she felt that Tom understood.

A silence hung over the darkening kitchen, broken at last by Tom saying heartily and quite unexpectedly, "Well now, Sarah, we've just got time to take Robin into the orchard and show her our surprise; shall we?"

Sarah's quick smile beamed out again, all weariness flown. "Yes, let's! She'll be pleased, won't she, Dad?"

Once more the chair was pushed into the yard. Robin offered to help, but understood at once that Tom was using the support of the chair to help him walk on his injured leg. She respected his determination and followed silently behind.

Sarah was giggling and twisting about in her seat. Suddenly, it was evident that she could keep the secret no longer. "Eeee-ore!" she shouted, the high little voice echoing around the buildings. And immediately there came a reply — the anguished wail that Robin remembered from her stay at the Black Dog . . . Chatterbox!

Tom halted at the entrance to a small

orchard just beyond the meal-house, and there stood the donkey, sad eyes watching expectantly as a couple of carrots were produced from Tom's pockets and given to Sarah to offer on the flat of her upturned palm.

"Well!" said Robin, flummoxed into silence. "And when did he arrive?"

"Yesterday." Tom watched his daughter stroke the shaggy head through the bars of the gate with a gentle, loving expression on his face that made Robin's heart race. "I knew, the gypsies wouldn't keep him, if they have to leave."

Robin winced, and Tom's alert eyes flew back to her. "*If*, I said," he repeated, with a quick return of the animosity she recalled so vividly. "Not *when* . . . I'm still fighting to keep Sentry House standing, you know."

She nodded, holding her tongue, and allowing the awkward moment to pass. "It's good of you," she said quietly after a moment.

"Method in my madness." Suddenly his voice rang with obstinacy. "I want Sarah to learn to ride the old moke. Someone told me that handicapped children often respond well to animals. I thought it was worth a try."

Curiously she wondered if her own ideas on the subject had entered his mind in some inexplicable way. It was strange that they could be on opposing sides and yet share so many thoughts.

Sarah was whispering fondly to Chatterbox, and Tom looked directly into Robin's wondering eyes. "I'm sorry you had such a rough time as a child," he said compassionately. "But perhaps you can make up for it now — you're welcome here at Well Farm, Robin, remember that. We're a poor substitute for a family of your own, I daresay — but, well, we'd like you to come and see us. Often."

She let out her tense breath in a quiet, slow sigh. What could she say to such an invitation? No words came and instead she put out a hand, unsure of what she was doing or of what his response might be, but unable to help herself.

He took it immediately between his own, raising her chill fingers to his lips. She shivered as she felt the warmth of his brief kiss, and then, as Sarah turned to say something, he released her.

The three of them talked brightly and happily as they returned to the house, but Tom's eyes constantly flickered towards her, and their shoulders brushed as they walked side by side behind Sarah's chair.

Janet met them at the kitchen door, her eyes as hostile as ever, and her thin face unsmiling. "Will she — Miss Ford — be staying for supper? If so I'll have to get some more meat out of the freezer — "

Awkwardly, Robin forced herself to look at Tom. He was clearly angry, but his vivid eyes held a reluctant twinkle. Fearing a flare-up of his quick temper, she said smoothly, before he could answer, "Indeed no, thanks — I must be off. I've got a — an appointment in Exeter. It's been lovely to see you Sarah — thanks for letting me come to your party. Tom — "

"Take Sarah in, Janet, will you?" His voice was rough, and as he accompanied Robin out of the yard to her car, he said contritely, "Damn the woman, will she never learn any manners? I'm sorry Robin, I'll speak to her about it . . . "

"Oh, please, no! She's quite entitled to feel how she likes about me, surely. I don't mind."

They looked at each other searchingly through the semi-darkness of the encroaching evening. "Thank you for coming," he said at last, frowning as if he meant to say more, but didn't know where to start.

Feelings flooded her, and she bent to unlock the door, trying to keep her face hidden from him. "And thank you — for everything, Tom."

Suddenly, he put his arms about her, pulling her around to face him. "Robin — must you go?" He grinned appealingly. "Damn Janet and the meat from the freezer — but stay for supper, won't you? Please?"

She opened her mouth to answer, but no sound came forth. If only she *could* stay — part of the family, he'd said, and oh, how the thought swelled inside her. Even Janet's unfriendly manner could be forgotten in the warmth and openhearted welcome of Tom and Sarah's affections.

But she remembered, wretchedly, that

Guy waited at Exeter, and she had still to make up her mind what answer to give him.

Out of the past, the childish barrier of flippancy arose again, something she had built as a defensive shell when things hurt her. Now it automatically sprang back into action as pain increased. She smiled at Tom brightly — too brightly — and got into the Mini.

"Sorry," she said airily through the open window, as she slipped the key into the ignition. "But I don't think Janet's meat from the freezer can really compete with a super dinner at the White Stag, can it? Another time, maybe Tom — and now, I really must go. Look after your leg. Cheerio!"

She drove off with the smile set on her face like a stiff mask, seeing in the mirror his astonished expression retreat into the darkening distance.

She thought of Tom, and she thought of Sentry House, and both things merged into appalling pain. Driving rapidly along the road to Exeter, Robin fumbled in her bag for a hanky and wondered if her heart really would break.

★ ★ ★

She drove on steadily and carefully, but part of her mind was engaged in a series of questions and answers which were at times revealing and hurtful. She knew she had grown fond of Tom, and yet she had deliberately upset him by parting so casually, almost flinging his invitation and warmth back into his face. Remembering, she winced and hated herself. The emotions that filled her threatened to overpower her flagging self-control; panic arose inside her, and then after it came new determination. It was disastrous to consider falling in love with Tom Hewitt — they were as different as chalk from cheese. Such a relationship would be doomed to failure from the start.

Now, Guy Devenish was much more her sort of man, no doubt of it — sophisticated, business-like, hard-living . . . if she took up his suggestion of a closer friendship she knew the sort of world she would be moving in: her own world of urban life, of social niceties and culture. Of money, and of the undoubted pleasure of an affluent life in white South Africa.

Whereas Tom was only a Devon farmer . . .

The cruel thought shocked her, and suddenly an image of his disbelieving, wounded stare caught at her heart with anguish and passion, and she shouted aloud to the passing shadowy trees and hedges — "But I'm doing this for his own good! Why can't he understand? Guy will let Sentry House stay as it is if I say yes to him!"

But still she saw Tom's face and the hurt surprise in his wide, vulnerable eyes.

It took all of her self-control to at last remove that clinging image from her mind's eye. But once she had done so, it seemed that there was no going back in memory, and immediately her thoughts became more optimistic. It was not so hard as she had initially imagined to anticipate Guy's welcoming smile when she reached the White Stag; almost enjoyable to guess how he would react when she told him her decision. Because, of course, there was only one course open to her now — she would say yes to him.

Yes, it was surprisingly easy; but she must never let herself think of Tom — not ever again.

By the time the twenty minute drive was ending, Robin was firmly set in her course of action. Realistically, she had finally succeeded in pushing all emotion behind her. She had ceased to be confused, unsure as to which of the two men she loved; now she was able to hide her inner feelings behind the efficient business mask which she had developed over the years, finding sufficient strength to treat Guy's proposition matter of factly, weighing up the benefits and disadvantages as if it were little more than a trade contract, and, when accepting the better deal, feeling at last eager to meet him and to find out what exactly he had in mind.

Perhaps, in her heart of hearts, she hoped vaguely that he wouldn't want to be tied down in marriage; perhaps, subconsciously, she still hoped that there might be a loophole — but she parked the Mini in the Cathedral Close and went into the hotel with her head held high and a look of determined acceptance on her face.

Guy was waiting in the foyer, his tense expression lightening as she entered.

"You're here!" The relief in his voice, and the warmth of his smile unexpectedly moved her. He wasn't, after all, the hard, relentless tycoon she had built up in her imagination during the drive here — no, he was just Guy, who was growing to understand her, to know how she thought, sensing what she needed. So she smiled back at him, words abruptly banished, and he put his arm around her in a brief caress.

Then the smile became lighter, and the familiar, masterful tone entered his voice again. "I had a nasty moment when I realised you'd walked out on me this morning . . . until I got your note. And even then — "

She looked at him as they entered the bar, finding a quiet spot in the corner of the room. "You didn't think I would keep my word? But I said I would be back."

There was a suggestion of reproof in

her voice and he looked almost humble as he nodded. "Sorry, my sweet — I should have known, of course. But I was afraid — that perhaps something might stop you: some*one*, perhaps . . . " His curious eyes grew sharp and watchful.

Tom, she thought numbly; *he knows about Tom. Is it so obvious? But it mustn't be — I won't let it be.* Aloud, she said carefully, "Well, I'm here, Guy; isn't that proof enough that — that nothing, no one, stopped me?"

"Sorry," he said again. "But you see, love, you've become very important to me. I need to be sure there's no competition. I want you for myself, no strings, no ties." He looked at her questioningly and behind the bright assurance of his handsome smile she sensed a vulnerability she hadn't known existed until now. The idea was an endearing one. So Guy wasn't as sure of himself as he seemed . . . suddenly it was easy to smile back, saying gently, "You must believe me, Guy — if there was competition, as you call it, I would hardly have come back, now would I?"

He took her hand, gripping it hard,

and again she was touched by the obvious depth of his feelings.

"Then perhaps this is the right moment for us to talk — to discuss the future."

"I'd like that. We've both got a decision to make, as I understand it, Guy."

"No. Wrong, love. You're the one with the decision ahead of you — mine's already made. And it's as strong as a rock."

She frowned, wondering. "I don't think I quite understand — "

Releasing her hand he sat back and watched her puzzled face with a tense expression in his eyes. "I'm asking you to do me the honour of marrying me, Robin, my love . . . "

Her heart turned over. This wasn't at all the scene she had anticipated. A formal proposal of marriage? Somehow the whole thing took on a ludicrous air, and weakly she began to laugh, stopping suddenly as she saw his face change.

"I didn't mean to be funny, sweetheart — but, of course, if you want the full treatment, I'll do the job properly, and get down on my knees . . . " He made a tentative move to get up from his chair and, not knowing if he really meant it, she put out a hand to stop him.

"Don't be so silly! It's not the done thing nowadays to make such a formal proposal — you must be very out of date in your part of the world!"

They laughed together, eyes clinging, and suddenly the mirth drained out of her; "Oh, Guy . . . " she dropped her hand to the table, holding it out to him, uncertain, a little afraid, but liking him more than she had ever thought possible.

His touch on her hand was warm and reassuring, his voice quiet, as he said, "Take it gently, darling. No need to look so worried. I'm not a bluebeard, you know. But I just wanted to tell you — I love you, Robin, my sweet girl, and I'll do all I can to make you happy if you'll only say yes . . . "

That quietly good-humoured under-standing was his saving grace; Robin knew, wildly, that if he had pushed her in any way, made his voice hectoring, his hands demanding, she would have refused him without a second thought. But because his perception warmed

191

her, she knew, too, that she must respond sincerely to his honourable, complimentary proposal.

She listened to the huskiness of her unsteady voice as if she were a stranger answering him. "Thank you, Guy. Believe me, I do appreciate what you've said. But — I'm still — not quite sure . . . " Suddenly, her resolution was weakening; the decision she had made in the car was no longer as strong as she remembered. There must be another way out . . . she began to fumble desperately for words. "Please, give me a little more time. After all, this would be a very big step for me — I mean, not just marriage, but giving up my job, my home, leaving England . . . it needs to be thought about very seriously."

"Of course. Marriage isn't anything to go into lightly. I've always had doubts myself before. One needs to be quite, quite sure . . . and we haven't known one another very long, have we? But it's been long enough for *me* — " He stared deep into her eyes and she wondered at the way his voice broke, as if he wished to say more but thought better of it. It was almost as if he read the reason for her hesitant excuses in her cloudy eyes, she thought wretchedly.

Then she remembered Sentry House and the peaceful atmosphere of Sennerton, too easily shattered, and was able to steel her wavering heart. "A week, Guy, please?"

"Very well. Seven days. I shall be back in town by then, anyway, so let's make a date . . . " He leaned back in his chair and became businesslike, noting down their meeting in his diary. "I shall have had time by then to find an estate agent who can perhaps find a local buyer for the old house — someone who won't put the village's back up, as you suggested. Hard luck for Harman, I know, but a bargain's a bargain. I've never welched on my word yet, and I don't intend to start now. We'll meet again in a week, eh? I'll ring you when I get to town and we'll have dinner. So that's decided. Now let's have a drink to seal the bargain, shall we? Won't be long, my sweet — don't disappear again, will you?"

He moved to the bar and she was alone. She stared at the vase of early daffodils that decorated the table. The fragile yellow blossoms were paper-thin and flagging in the heat of the room: they looked — and were — out of their element.

She touched a drooping petal tenderly, and knew a moment of shocked truth. *You should be growing in a field somewhere; and I should be at Well Farm, with Tom and Sarah.*

But there could be no going back now. She wondered briefly, with a nagging sense of misery, whether, however much attracted she was to Guy, she would love him enough to make their marriage a happy one? He deserved to be happy.

11

GUY came back from the bar with a smile that lit up his whole face. "I've ordered champagne," he said happily. "Only the best for us tonight, my darling. Oh yes, I know you haven't actually accepted me yet" — as Robin's smile abruptly fled and her eyes clouded over — "but I'm hoping. Isn't there an old saying about it — something like I breathe I hope . . . well, that's how I feel right now."

"I didn't know you were so romantic — "

"There's a lot you don't know about me; give us time and we'll both find out how we tick." He watched the waiter pouring the champagne, and then, once they were alone again, lifted his glass to touch hers. "To us, Robin. To our future — together." His deepset eyes held hers for a long, silent moment, as they sipped the sparkling wine.

She put down her glass thoughtfully. "You make me feel very small and ashamed of myself, Guy — you know very well that I tried to blackmail you over the business of Sentry House, and yet you're taking it so marvellously. I — I really do appreciate your understanding . . . "

"And you're surprised by it? Yes, you are, I can see it written all over your face! You thought I was just another bloody-minded businessman with an eye to the main chance, I suppose!"

She smiled, a little sadly, and nodded. "Well, you did rather give that impression, you know — just at first."

"But now you know the truth, that I'm an old softie at heart." He laughed and then became abruptly serious. "Don't we all build shells to protect ourselves from hurt and disappointment? Of course we do. I've seen *your* protective shell, just as you've seen mine. It's a good thing that we can talk about it. You see, I feel we're two of a kind in many ways." He refilled her glass. "Drink up."

"I don't think so, thanks . . . "

"Nonsense. This is an evening to remember! Let yourself go for once — you've got a nice comfortable bed awaiting you up on the second floor, and if necessary I'll carry you up there! Come on, just a drop more . . . "

The second glass made her nose prickle and sent a glorious feeling of carelessness into her tired mind and body. He was right, she admitted to herself as the pleasant sensation took hold of her, she had no responsibilities to anyone tonight, so why not enjoy the moment?"

Something he'd just said intrigued her. "You mentioned my protective shell — "

He signalled a hovering waiter. "Let's discuss that over our dinner, shall we, my darling? And we'll take the champagne with us."

In the large, elegant dining room they ate a delicious meal and talked freely all through it. Robin discovered that two glasses of champagne was a most delightfully painless method of dispelling her worries and, by the end of the meal, was chattering without a care in the world.

Fondly, Guy told her that he had known, right from the start, that her crisp, business-like attitude hid a very vulnerable and sensitive inner Robin — "and it's that nice soft girl inside you that I find so appealing, my darling. Let's be honest, I've met so many of the other types — the Girl Fridays who can wipe the floor with you, and do so at the drop of a hat, the business women who have forgotten what femininity means . . . so it's a joy to find someone like you who combines all the qualities a man really wants in a wife."

When, finally, they parted at bedtime, she allowed him to accompany her upstairs to her door, even finding it difficult to deny him entry once he took her in his arms and kissed her goodnight, a kiss that became longer and more demanding as the minutes fled.

At last she pushed him away, saying, laughing and breathless, "That's enough, Guy! It's not fair to take advantage of me because I've had too much champagne! Let's call it a day, shall we?"

"I'd much rather call it a night — but if that's how you want it, then I won't argue. Goodnight, my sweetheart — you know, don't you, that the next seven days and nights are going to be the longest of my life?"

He kissed her again, gently and with infinite tenderness, before leaving her.

As she shut the bedroom door behind her Robin felt she was floating on air; but next morning, waking early because of the traffic in the Close, the sense of euphoria had completely gone, and she was faced with the memory of her unthinking behaviour the previous evening.

Had she unfairly encouraged him? If so, it was merely the damned champagne he had persuaded her to drink, and therefore as much his fault as hers. She thought ruefully that she had been foolish to allow herself to get so carried away; and yet they had learned so many things about each other — on her part, not least, the fact that Guy was more sweet and understanding than she had ever imagined — that she could hardly write off the evening as a disaster.

Guy. Tom. Sentry House. The words went around in her brain like a millrace, and the problem hung in the air as she dressed and went down to have her breakfast, hoping desperately that she could get away before he appeared. By the time she was in the car she was no nearer an answer, but now one thought alone was pre-dominant in her mind, and she headed the Mini back in the direction of Sennerton instead of driving straight to London.

It was vitally important to return to the village, on her own, without any more issues clouding her vision. She had no wish to see Guy, or Tom, or even Manny or Sarah . . . Sentry House was the only thing that called her, for a last long, assessing look, to discover if a building, even as old and beautiful as Sentry undoubtedly was, was really worth the sacrifice she planned to make on its behalf.

Somehow, as she drove, the idea of the problem's resolution lying there in the village increased, and when she reached Sennerton she had no eyes for anyone or anything other than the entrance to the house.

She drove past the 'van and the summerhouse without even wondering if Manny was still skiving off school, and when she parked close to the crumbling walls of the house she got out immediately, almost mesmerised by the hold the place had on her.

Sentry House meant so much to her; there was no reason why it should, but deep inside her the feeling grew and grew. It *must* be kept standing; Tom was so right, the way he felt . . . abruptly his name threatened to undermine her determination once again, but she pushed the thought away fiercely, and stared up at the facade before her, trying to imprint the character of the gilding on to her mind for ever, because, of course, she would never return here once the decision was made and carried out.

The time passed without her knowledge, so deep was her absorption, and only when she noticed something blocking the light behind her as she wandered inside among the desolate, empty rooms, did she start and turn around, suddenly thrust back into the present from a world of evocative memories and imaginings.

Her heart missed a beat. Nip Lee faced her, his eyes wild and his mouth as grim as a steel trap. "So *you're* 'ere, are you? Come fer a last look before it all comes down, eh?"

She backed away, sudden fear making her tense and stiff. He smelt of whisky and had obvious trouble keeping steady on his feet. The fact that he was drunk added to her anxiety: Nip sober was bad enough, but like this he could well be dangerous. Carefully, and without openly seeming to, she inched towards a doorway behind her. He was in a menacing mood and she had no illusions about her safety should it suddenly enter his head to attack her. Perhaps she could get out of the room and out the back way . . .

But Nip, with surprising enterprise, headed her off, stumbling to the door and rocking there on his heels, grinning wolfishly.

"Got you, my fine lady! No sneaking out that way — no, no, you an' I got a little problem to work out . . . "

She summoned all her courage. "What problem is that, then, Nip?"

"Why, this ole house, o'course. Think I'm gonna let you go, after all you've done to help knock it down? Oh, no!" He came unsteadily towards her, the foolish grin fading into a wild scowl.

She wasn't silly enough to think she could argue with him; excuses would only make matters worse and he was in no condition to understand the actual truth of the matter. The best idea seemed to be to go along with him, agree with whatever he said, keep him occupied and then — with luck — slip away and escape to safety.

Casting her eyes around the big room, she noticed once again the initials engraved on the far window, and suddenly hope gave her fresh confidence. "Have you ever seen this, Nip? Look, behind you, over there on the window . . . oh, but of course you must have! I mean, you know this house so well, and all its history— perhaps you can tell me who scratched that initial there — shall we go over and have a look?"

He narrowed his wild eyes. "You're tryin' to get round me — "

"Of course I'm not: it's just that you've been here in the village a long time, so you can tell me something I don't know about the house. Do come over here, Nip, please — "

Holding her breath, boldly she stepped forward, passing him, smiling brightly as she did so, then turning her back on him, praying that her scheme would work and that his fuddled mind would forget his threats against her.

For a few stretching seconds there was no sound, and fears raced through her anew; was he even now gathering himself to rush at her? But then his stumbling feet made a board creak and she turned, slowly, so as not to alarm him further. "Here it is, on the window pane. I wonder who PD was? It's very old, well over two hundred years . . . can you think who it might have been?"

She heard her heart pumping wildly, and tried to think up something else with which to divert him; but then he was staggering towards her, to stop, glaring blindly up at the window. He frowned ferociously. "What initial? I can't see nothin' . . . " Suddenly he lowered his head like a bull and began shouting. "You're trickin' me, that's what you're doing! You fine lady, you, with yer posh voice and yer London ways, we don't want you here, we don't — and I'm gonna make sure you don't never come back . . . "

He was upon her before the thick

words finished pouring out, hands heavy around her neck, filling her with terror and pain, and the smell of him making her feel sick. "Let me go! No, Nip, no . . . !"

Her scream petered out as the pressure tightened, and she wondered desperately if she was to die here in Sentry House, at the hands of a drunken gypsy who actually loved the old house as she did hers — Surely, she thought hysterically, fate couldn't allow such a ridiculous thing to happen . . .

Through her wild thoughts she became aware of other voices shouting, of a familiar face appearing at Nip's back; thankfully she watched strong hands pull his arms away from her.

Charlie Lee, with a face of thunder, yelled, "Get off Nip, you stupid bastard — ," and threw his brother to the floor, where he lay in a moaning heap.

Robin touched her bruised throat and wondered if she was going to faint. Then Charlie put a huge arm around her shoulders and growled, "Let's get you into the open, away from here . . . "

Before she could reply, he had swept

her off her feet and strode out of the house. In the drive, the cold wind revived her, and she was able to smile a little as she murmured hoarsely, "Thank you, Charlie — am I glad you came just then! I'll be all right now; yes, honestly, I can stand up . . . "

He put her down as gently as if she were his own child, and stood staring at her, with concern heavy on his face. "I never wanted fer anything like this to happen, Miss — you must believe me; I'll shout fer me rights like anyone, but this — oh, that stupid bastard, I'll kill him fer this!"

Robin wanted to laugh, but hadn't the strength. Soothingly, she said, "I think one act of violence is quite enough for this morning, Charlie — so don't do anything rash, will you? Poor old Nip must be feeling pretty bad as it is — I should think it'll take some time for his head to cool down, and I'm sure he'll be sorry when he's sobered up."

Charlie's face froze. "You mean you're gonna forget it? Not go to the police, or anything?"

"Certainly not. That would only make

more trouble in the village on my account; honestly, Charlie, I never wanted any of this to happen." She looked up at him pleadingly, and to her surprise he suddenly smiled and patted her awkwardly on the shoulder. Gruffly, he said, "I know that now, Miss. We was all a bit angry-like when first you come, but, well I know what sort of a lady you are now, see? And me and Brit, well we know how good you bin to Manny, little devil . . . mind you — " His frown returned momentarily, but she saw a twinkle in the black eyes, even as he went on fiercely, "Mind you, I shall still shout fer me rights, like I said! No one's gonna knock down old Sentry House, not while I'm around. So if I was you, Miss, I'd get back in your car and run along. I'll see to Nip, and by the time I've finished with him he won't never try any tricks any more . . . you sure you're all right, now?"

Robin took a deep breath and saw the wisdom of his suggestion. She held out her hand and smiled at him.

"I'm fine, Charlie, thanks, and I'm so glad that we're friends, after all. Tell

Nip — tomorrow, not now — that I understand why he was so angry with me; but please explain that actually we're both on the same side. You see, now that I've got to know Sennerton and the old house, I can't bear to think of anything changing. And it won't change, Charlie — I can almost promise you that."

He stared, her hand forgotten in his. "You mean it's all bin a mistake? It's not gonna be made into something new?"

"Not exactly a mistake — just a plan that hasn't worked. And I think you can take it that a new plan will only mean the restoration of Sentry."

"Well, that's better! Best news I've heard for a long time!"

Together they walked towards the Mini and she got in, suddenly glad to sit down, but feeling strangely calm, despite the awful memory of Nip's fingers around her neck. "Give my regards to your wife, Charlie, will you? And my love to Manny; tell him I'll be in touch sometime . . . Goodbye now."

" 'Bye, Miss."

She threw him a last watery smile and then drove away from Sentry House, passing the summerhouse and the 'van with her eyes averted leaving the village and refusing to allow herself to look behind for one last glance.

The morning's frightening episode had made up her mind, once and for all. She had told Charlie that Sentry House would continue standing, and there was to be no going back on the decision, so hardly made.

It was heart-breaking leaving the gently billowing countryside of Devon, and knowing that for her it was now forbidden territory. In future she would, no doubt, see more beautiful landscapes, and experience other pleasant life-styles, but she knew with a sad certainty that none of them would in any way compare with the love she had for the twisting lanes and the high hedges of the county she was now leaving.

So, in one way, it was a great relief to turn on to the motorway and follow the stretching conveyor belt of traffic back to London and the flat that must, once again, be her home.

12

THE Ealing flat was strangely lonely, because of the suggestion of Manny's remembered presence. She steeled herself to be busy, catching up on neglected chores and so not allowing herself time to think. She had done what had to be done — given Guy a promise that she would consider his proposal — dully she knew her mind was now inevitably made up. She would say yes at the end of the week, when next she saw him, and they would be married as soon as possible — by special licence, perhaps — so that they could leave for South Africa without further delay.

It would be fatal to have regrets now. She was half-way to loving Guy, and he had said that he loved her. And he would keep his side of the bargain, she was sure of it: Sentry House would be sold to a conservative new owner who would be happy to merely restore the old place, perhaps even accepting words of advice from the village as he did so, and peace would return to Sennerton.

And at Well Farm Sarah would grow and be happy, for surely, with medical science expanding its knowledge so widely, she would soon be released from her wheelchair? There was such vitality in the child, it was impossible to think of her remaining a cripple all her life.

Robin found herself willing Sarah to grow strong. At such moments it was hard not to think of Tom as well; but her icy self-control became stronger as the days passed, and gradually his disturbing image faded before the onslaught of her intent determination, into the uneasy memory of an irritating man with a passion to have his own autocratic way about Sentry House.

Only one more day to go, Robin told herself as the week flew by and she arrived at the office on the Friday morning. It would be a huge relief to meet Guy tomorrow and give him his answer — she would feel that the frustrating waiting time was over, and some decisive action would help her to get on with her new life, forgetting the old. Although, right from the start she had been determined to say yes, the lapse of time had inevitably brought niggles of doubt and uncertainty with it, and she was tense and brittle still because of the pressure of her conflicting thoughts. She wished tomorrow would quickly come.

Derek's irate voice shouted down the corridor as she arrived at the office. "Where's Miss Ford? Isn't she here yet? Tell her I want her as soon as she comes in — why does she have to be late, this morning of all days?"

Cleo's flushed face told its own tale. "Mr Harman says . . . "

"Yes, I heard him, Cleo, thanks." Robin's smile was tight. She wasn't in the mood for Derek's tantrums. "I'm on my way."

She knocked at his half-open door.

"Oh, it's you? At last." He wore the badgered looked that meant things had gone wrong over the Midlands deal: problems had been building up all the week, and Robin guessed that he was about to use her as a whipping-post, ready to undam all his fury on her innocent shoulders.

Once — before the Sennerton contract had cropped up — she would have accepted the situation and laughed him gently out of his ill-humour. This morning, though, it was the last straw, about to break the camel's back. She tilted her chin and met his aggrieved eyes with a cold, hard resistance.

"You're late," he growled.

"Only one minute. St. John's over the way has just struck nine, I heard it on the way up."

They glared at each other, then Derek crashed back his chair and aced around the room like a frustrated tiger. "That blasted man, Devenish — he's pulled out of the Sennerton contract." His narrowed eyes gleamed at her fretfully.

"Yes."

He made an explosive noise, stopping short in his enraged pacing. "You know, do you? Why didn't you tell me, then?"

"I wasn't sure — although it was fairly certain. I thought it best to let him tell you himself. After all, you did take the job out of my hands." She enjoyed his quick scowl of guilty annoyance.

"Trust a woman to bring up that sort of thing! Well, I blame you for the whole caboosh — if you hadn't mishandled matters right from the beginning, everything would have been signed and sealed by now. You're responsible for losing me a hefty profit, my girl."

It was too much. Robin felt a surge of selfrighteous anger and said quickly, "How dare you! That's a lot of nonsense and you know it, Derek! It's nothing at all to do with me that Guy has decided not — not to — " She stopped abruptly, her own words ringing false in her ears.

Derek stared. "What's the matter? Run out of excuses?"

Numbly she met his eyes, feeling colour rush to her cheeks as the truth of the matter revealed itself and her guilt grew. "I'm sorry," she muttered, after a pause. "I hadn't quite realised what I was saying. In a way, you see, it's true — it *is* because of me that Guy has decided not to sell you Sentry House — oh, I can't explain, you wouldn't understand! But he's asked me to marry him, and so . . . "

"*Marry* you?" Derek exploded into

white hot rage. "You mean you're blackmailing the poor chap? Making him give up Sentry House, letting it rot where it stands? Oh yes, that's what you wanted, didn't you? You and your pathetic urge to keep the damned village happy! And so you held out a carrot, which the poor sap's taken . . . and I'm several thousands worse off because of it! My God, Robin, you're no good to me any longer, now you've started doing that sort of thing . . . "

She swallowed and knew the wretchedness of hearing truth twisted into believable falsity. She wanted to argue, to explain, to make Derek understand, but the expression on his contorted face was hardly encouraging. She decided that a dignified retreat was all that was left to her — and quickly, before she made a fool of herself.

She made it short and sharp, heading for the door as she spoke. "I'm sorry, Derek, I really am. You're wrong in some of the things you're thinking — everything isn't as black and white as you imagine — but let's leave it at that. Of course, I'll give you my resignation: I'll tidy my desk and go — it's better that way, isn't it? Well — goodbye — "

"Good*bye*!" He followed her to the door, slamming it vehemently behind her as she went down the corridor.

Robin reeled back to her own office, feeling she had been torn apart by a particularly powerful whirlwind. Luckily her work was up-to-date. She gave some last instructions to Cleo, gathered together her personal belongings and left the building.

Now, more than ever, was it impressed upon her that marriage to Guy was the only sure thing left in this seemingly unpredictable world. As if in a trance, she negotiated the streaming traffic, driving back to the flat. Hardly had she shut the front door than the phone bleeped in the hall and she answered it automatically, her thoughts still far away, her mind shocked by the remembrance of Derek's livid face.

"Robin?"

For a moment she just stood there, not believing; then a great spontaneous rush of joy thrust through her. Trembling, she grasped at the chair beside the telephone. "Oh, Tom — !"

He sounded a very long way off. The line crackled and his indistinct voice was stern and upset. Robin's joy turned to anxiety.

"I phoned your office and they said you weren't there. Not ill, are you?"

Weakly, remembering all that had just happened, she tried to smile. "No, I'm not ill."

"Can't hear you — are you there, Robin?"

"Yes, Tom, I'm here. How — how are you?"

"What? Speak up, can't you? Now look, I can't waste time, there's too much to do. But I want you to come down here first thing tomorrow morning. I've got several things to tell you."

"Tom, what's it all about? I can't just leave everything and come down . . . "

"Of course you can. Good grief, Robin, it's important! Get that into your head! I wouldn't ring at this hour of the day if it wasn't, what with phone rates so high . . . "

In spite of her confusion, she smiled.

Dear Tom! So full of admirable virtues beneath his outbursts and passions. "Can't you tell me a bit more?"

"Damn this line! It sounds as if someone's fiddling with the wires. Robin — can you hear me? Come tomorrow, early. There's a seven forty-five train, I looked it up, it'll be quicker than driving. You *must* come . . . "

"Really, Tom, I don't think there's any point in — "

Then the line went dead and she didn't know whether he had slammed down the receiver, or whether the wire had been disconnected.

She went into the kitchenette and made some coffee sitting quietly, with her muddled thoughts roaming in many directions. What a hopeless chaos her world was in; just when she'd succeeded in putting him out of her mind, abruptly, uninvited, Tom had come back, with a force that dismayed her.

How on earth had she ever imagined she could entirely forget him and marry Guy? It was an utter impossibility, and as the day wore on she accepted the hard truth of the matter, knowing that she must indeed see Tom again, even if it was only to give herself time to find a more constructive way out of the maze.

And yet — if she didn't accept Guy's proposal — what would happen to Sentry House! Even more important — what would happen to Tom? Violence had been aimed at him once as it had at her; it could, and probably would, happen again. And it would be all her fault.

Sighing, in no way sure of what she was doing, Robin went to the phone. She dialled the hotel where Guy stayed in town. His deep, confident voice touched her heartstrings. It was so unfair, asking him to wait even longer for her reply — how could she be so hurtful, liking him as she did? But she had to have time; had to see what Tom wanted of her.

"Oh, Guy, it's me — Robin."

"Hallo, my sweet."

She panicked at the intimate warmth of his voice. "Er — something's cropped up, something very urgent. I'm afraid I have to — er — go away tomorrow, just for the day. So could we postpone our date? I'll phone you again when I get back again . . . "

A chuckle surprised her. "I suppose this urgency couldn't possibly be anything to do with Sentry House? Has the grapevine been at work?"

She was too taken aback to reply. What did he mean?

"Robin? Did you hear what I said?"

"Y — yes. Yes, I heard. But how do you know? What's happened to Sentry House? I mean — "

"My sweet girl, I was just about to ring you myself and tell you the news, only you've beaten me to it." He paused, clearly enjoying her silent anticipation. "Sentry is up for auction, it seems . . . tomorrow at noon. I heard from the agent this morning. We'll drive down together. If we leave early we'll be there in good time."

Foolishly she murmured some inadequate comment, and then found a hasty excuse not to see him later in the day. "I've got a lot to do, Guy — work, you know — and then, what with getting ready for tomorrow . . . " She hated herself for the deception, but knew she couldn't face an evening with him, feeling as she did.

Tomorrow would be the irrevocable test; when she must set Guy beside Tom at the auction. She would have to decide then, once and for all.

Her mind wandered after she'd put the phone down. So the fate of dear old Sentry House was to be settled tomorrow; clearly, Guy had kept his word, and the local agent must have found at least two prospective buyers. She frowned. But why had Tom sounded so urgent, demanding that she must be at the sale? Surely he realised that the fate of the old house was no longer anything to do with her?

Robin's head swam, as fact and fancy intertwined restlessly. But one clear thought impressed itself upon her, above the chaos of confused emotions, hopes and anxieties.

She knew that more than the fate of Sentry House would be at stake tomorrow. The stage was set for something vast and dramatic, and she, Guy and Tom would be the principal actors, playing the scene to its end.

★ ★ ★

Guy was silent as they drove towards Exeter the next morning. Robin, her thoughts busy as she sat beside him, watching the countryside slip past, was uncertain of his mood. Was he cross with her for some reason? Or worried about the outcome of the sale? Perhaps merely concentrating on his driving . . . it entered her head with dismal truth that, after all, she hardly knew him.

True, he had greeted her with his usual warmth when they met at her flat earlier. "We're in good time," he had said, pleasantly enough, as he settled her into the passenger seat of the gleaming maroon Porsche and adjusted her seatbelt. "No problems."

She reflected on his words as the journey progressed. Even if he anticipated no problems, she was all too well aware of them.

Suppose no one wanted Sentry House badly enough to offer a price that would reach the reserve Guy had almost certainly put on the property? How terribly responsible she would feel. And if no buyer materialised at the sale, what then? What would Guy do? Most important of all, to Robin's anguished mind what would he expect of her in such a situation? Would he hold her to her side of the bargain? And could she agree to marry him, even if the issue of Sentry House remained unresolved?

She worried until mid-morning, when suddenly Guy nodded his head towards the south-west and said, "Dartmoor's ahead," and she saw the familiar, dramatic humps and bumps on the skyline that meant Sennerton was near. And then, strangely, as if the grandeur of the timeless landscape had put her anxieties into perspective and healed her aching apprehension, she knew that she must accept whatever happened at the sale, be it good or bad.

Why worry over things that might never happen! She was able, then, to relax and smile at Guy, saying quietly, "What a beautiful morning . . . "

The sun was bright in a mountainous sky of piled white clouds. Wind roared in the trees that dotted the village green as they got out of the car in Sennerton and Robin felt her cheeks begin to glow;

country air, what a tonic it was, both to mind and body.

And then, out of the blue, an urgent, endearing voice yelled behind her, "You're back! I said as you would be — me Mum had a funny turn this morning — saw a robin hiding it's head under it's wing, and I said, 'Pooh! that's no robin, that's *Miss*! She'll come fer the sale, see if she don't!'"

Robin's face broke into a smile of welcome as Manny's dark eyes stared adoringly at her. "That's not bad — hiding my head under my wing, was I? Well, that's exactly how I felt — until now. Oh, Manny, it super to see you again!"

"Course you are. Can't do without me, can you?" Cockily, he danced ahead of them as she and Guy approached the village hall at the far end of the long, narrow street. "Lots of ole geysers here already. I bin standing around for hours, waiting for you to come. I seen everyone so far — dealers, agents, buyers; cor, if you wants to know who's who, jest ask!"

Guy's eyebrows lifted, exchanging

an unseen glance with Robin. "Quite the little walking encyclopaedia," he commented dryly. "You certainly seem to have a fatal fascination for the male population of the village, my darling."

She smiled back, but wondered at the implication in his words. He knew about Tom, of course — and wasn't letting her forget that he knew.

Tom. She stared quickly around as they entered the hall. People milled about, some sitting chatting, some standing in groups. Voices rose and fell, and over the continuous drone she heard someone say loudly, "That's him — the one in the blue anorak. He owns the Victoria Hotel in Bushelhampton . . . had his eye on Sentry for ages, so I heard. Well, he's got his chance now. Wouldn't be bad if the old place were turned into a hotel, wouldn't change things too much, eh?"

Robin followed the neighbouring eyes that singled out the man in question, a large, fleshy man talking earnestly to the woman at his side; if the village knew him and approved, then surely Sentry House's fate could only be a happy one. She breathed more freely, full of new hope.

But there must be other would-be-buyers; casting around, she looked for likely candidates. Manny hovered at her side, eyes darting like a dragonfly as he, too, surveyed the crowd. She lowered her voice, bending towards him. "O.K. then, Mr Know-all — that's one of them, the chap on blue from the Victoria Hotel — who else is there?"

"Well, I reckons that one there could be . . . "

But Manny's pointing finger was hidden from her sight as a man suddenly stepped in front of her.

"Robin!" Tom Hewitt's eyes were vivid, full of a strange expression she hadn't seen before. His welcome was uninhibited and direct, and for a brief moment she forgot she was here as Guy's intended wife.

Tom grasped her hand, his infectious warmth seeming to flow into her, carrying with it a feeling of happiness and confidence. She murmured his name and allowed herself to relax in the knowledge that he was clearly very pleased to see her. There would be difficulties and possible heartbreak before the sale was finished, she knew; but for this one short moment she and Tom were together, and she was at ease. She was happy.

"I'm glad you've come. You're going to have a surprise when you know what's happened." His eyes never left her face and she felt the rest of the world draw away a little, leaving them alone and united.

"You sound as if everything was going to turn out all right — like the proverbial happy ending." Her voice trembled at the sudden hopelessness of it all, and his hands gripped hers even harder.

"Just wait and see! It could happen, you know . . . " He was smiling, and she thought she'd never seen this particular Tom Hewitt before; confident, masterful — it was a completely new aspect of him. She had known him charming and hateful, overbearing when he was angry, rude and defiant as passion swept him, even gentle and compassionate in moments with Sarah — but this Tom was the most exciting and lovable of all. Despite her natural anxiety over the outcome of the sale, his words made her almost believe what he said.

"A fairy tale ending? One that pleases everybody? The village, you, me, Guy? Come off it, Tom, life doesn't work out like that . . . " As she said Guy's name her smile faded, and she slid her hands out of Tom's grasp. Turning away, she said carefully, "Guy drove me down. He's concerned to see how the sale goes, of course."

"Of course." Tom's suddenly ice gaze fell upon Guy standing not far away, talking to a balding man holding a sheaf of papers. "That's Lovell, the estate agent — looks worried, doesn't he? I'm not surprised. He's got competition here that he didn't know about!"

Robin was caught by the optimistic tone of his words. "What do you mean, Tom?" She saw the fire in his eyes sparking out again, and instinctively guessed that he still had a card up his sleeve. "You've done something you're pleased about! Something no one else knows about! That's it, isn't it?"

Smiling down at her, he put an arm about her shoulders in a fleeting, rough caress. "That's it, my lovely! One in the eye for your Mr Devenish, not to mention that boss chap of yours. Look, I've got to run, I'm meeting someone very special at any moment. Keep your fingers crossed. Promise?"

"I promise, Tom — " She was left with the memory of his smile and his new confidence, standing in the crowded hall aware that for this little moment everything was beautiful. Then Guy came to her side and her heart leaped as guilt and quick anxiety flooded her anew. "Oh! I was just talking to Tom — Tom Hewitt — "

"I saw you."

She thought his voice was dry and disapproving, and so began to chatter on, trying desperately to dispel the sudden uneasiness between them. "What a lot of people! Shows how interested everyone is in the sale . . . "

"So it seems. Come and sit over here." There was no arguing with the hand beneath her elbow, and they settled themselves in the front row of chairs, facing a trestle table behind which stood more people with papers, busy tongues and keen, hopeful expressions.

Guy glanced at his watch impatiently.

"Come on," he said, half-aloud, and she realised that, in his own way, he was as worked up as she was.

Impulsively she touched his arm. "I hope you make a good sale; you've been so understanding about this, Guy — "

His steel-grey eyes relented as they lingered on her face. "You're a funny creature, Robin — too soft-hearted for your own good, sometimes." Then a reluctant smile appeared, and he pressed her fingers in his. "But thanks anyway. Ah look — I think we're really getting under way at last."

13

THE auctioneer took his seat, a signal for others to follow suit. His assistant passed files and plans to and fro down the table and then the wooden gavel sounded, demanding attention from the packed rows of seats.

"Ladies and gentlemen, we're here to offer a fine old property for public auction . . . " The auctioneer's brisk, impersonal voice began detailing Sentry Hall's impressive history and itemising its faded charms.

Robin looked carefully around her. Where was Tom? Her eyes swept the seats on either side, then she half turned, glancing rapidly at the back of the hall. A familiar profile caught her eyes; so Derek had come as well — she flinched. Any meeting with him was bound to be difficult, but she supposed it was something she couldn't avoid before the day was out. Then an unexpected glow of strength brought her head up — she would face him, come what may. Her conscience was quite clear, whatever he might suppose to the contrary.

Suddenly there was a commotion at the door, and a man's voice shouted roughly, "I've come to claim me rights! That there ole house has given us sanctuary for 'undreds of years — it ain't gonna stop now, not if I can help it . . . "

Heads turned and a hum of surprise drowned the auctioneer's words for a moment. Robin recognised Charlie Lee's burly form, struggling with a couple of hefty villagers. Behind him another face came into view — brother Nip, also shouting about his rights. Beneath the horror that she felt at such a display of emotional violence, Robin couldn't help appreciating the family ties that bound the two men together, despite their differences in the past over the fate of Sentry House.

As quickly as the row began, it was over; man-handled and out-numbered, the two gypsies were thrust outside the door, and once again the auctioneer resumed his task. But the point had been made, and Robin, like many another onlooker, felt the old village conflict re-focus, charging the atmosphere with greater awareness.

At the end of the auctioneer's description she waited, with mounting nervousness, for the bids to start. Now she would discover just who the prospective buyers were — and how many there were. Manny, for all his boasting, had known very little. Robin hung on the country voices as they slowly started bidding, and had no compunction in turning around to identify their owners.

"Fifteen thousand!" The man from the Victoria Hotel was smiling wickedly as he made the first ridiculous bid. The auctioneer's eyebrows raised and a flurry of suppressed laughter swept the hall.

"Fifteen thousand for Sentry House. Thank you, sir — can anyone manage a little more? The grounds alone are worth treble that figure . . . "

In the palpitating silence Robin heard Charlie still shouting outside and smiled to herself. She guessed he was trying to rouse village feelings, and then suddenly her nervousness increased — please God, let there be no more violence . . .

A light voice from the far end of the row said quietly, "Twenty-five thousand," and the hall buzzed with fresh interest. A feminine voice, pleasant, warm and well-spoken. Robin stared along the line of heads, all turned just as hers was, and saw the speaker, an attractively fair-haired woman wearing an expensive-looking town suit and elegant boots. She nodded confidently at the auctioneer as he repeated the bid.

Robin's heart faltered as she watched the woman lean sideways to the man sitting by her, smile and whisper something, to which he replied with an emphatic shake of the head and a look of determination: Tom Hewitt.

His words rang in Robin's memory, suddenly full of meaning. "I'm meeting someone very special — " She hardly heard the next bid from the man who owned the Victoria Hotel. In the murmur of voices all around her mind churned, fitting imaginary jigsaw pieces together. What a fool she had been to think that Tom had any real feeling for her; he'd merely been excited because of the sale and his freshly stimulated hope of keeping Sentry House intact — with the help of the attractive blonde. Excited, no doubt, because she was about to arrive; clearly the woman must be wealthy to consider buying such a property. A wretchedly unkind thought hit Robin like a body blow; was Tom selling himself to the blonde, for the sake of the old house?

Like you're selling yourself to Guy? suggested her grim conscience.

Numbly she sat there, not heeding the bids that now came briskly one after the other. The man from the Victoria Hotel, then the blonde. Robin stared straight ahead with eyes that threatened to flood with tears if she let go of her control for a second.

Guy glanced at her, and she felt his warm hand covering her icy fingers. "Cheer up," he murmured in her ear. "Looks as if I'll get my money, even now!"

She snatched her hand away, glaring back at him, shocked out of her misery, unable to recognise the dry humour in his voice. "Is that all you can think about — money?" she hissed, and had the satisfaction of seeing him blink in surprise.

"Don't be such a little fool — I was only joking — "

"Be quiet!" Suddenly she realised things had come to a head. The atmosphere in the hall was electric, everyone sitting on the edges of their seats. Which of the two prospective buyers would get Sentry House?

Now the auctioneer's voice was less impersonal, his words coloured by the growing climax of the sale. "One hundred and forty-five thousand! I'm bid a hundred and forty-five thousand by this gentleman — come along, Madam, you can't let a fine old property slip from your grasp now! Did I hear you make another bid, Madam?"

Silence hung like a heavy blanket and all eyes were focussed on the slim figure of the woman sitting so calmly beside Tom. Casually, she recrossed her legs and shifted the leather handbag on her lap. Then she glanced sideways at Tom, smiled reassuringly and said firmly and clearly, "One hundred and fifty thousand."

A response of "Oohs" swept the packed seats, and the man in the blue anorak relaxed in his chair, wiping his forehead and shaking his head. He turned to his companion, muttering, "That's it, then. Beyond me this time."

The auctioneer picked up his gavel and gave the required formula. "No more bids, ladies and gentlemen? Well then — going for one hundred and fifty thousand pounds . . . going, going GONE!" The hammer blow announced the end of the sale and immediately the hall was in noisy uproar.

Robin's tension snapped and she knew she would explode if she didn't get out. She slipped out of her seat, ignoring Guy, stumbling over feet and jostling people as she fled.

Familiar faces slid into her line of vision and then swiftly receded; Bert Woodall, looking worried and uncertain; Nip Lee and Charlie, one heavy face grinning, the other ashamed and apologetic. Janet, surprisingly full of smiles. Robin tripped against Janet's chair and was amazed when the once-hostile eyes met hers and beamed a huge smile. "Turned out all right then, didn't it, Miss Ford? What a relief . . . "

Unable to think straight, not knowing what Janet meant, Robin merely shook her head and went on towards the door. Behind her Manny shouted, but she took no notice. One thought filled her mind, one haven calling her. She ran out into the bright, cold mid-day sun, hardly knowing where she was going, yet allowing her legs to carry her on, trusting them to help her reach her inevitable destination.

Only when she was outside Sentry House did she stop, leaning against the old stone walls, her legs shaking and her head spinning. Slowly she entered the quiet shadows of the empty house, feeling a sort of peace gradually calm her disturbed mind.

She had come here, she realised suddenly, for sanctuary. Sanctuary, what Tom had been fighting for, Charlie and Nip shouting about. The thought made her understand that it was indeed right for Sentry House to continue standing, not to be redeveloped as Guy had planned. And yet, what would the blonde woman do with it, now it was hers? Robin knew bitterly, yet resignedly, that she would probably do whatever Tom asked of her; and so Sentry House was safe.

The knowledge of having done the right thing, despite all her anxieties and doubts, swept over her. Sennerton's future was more important than her own; at that moment a strange stab of intuition hinted that maybe her future *was* Sennerton's, after all, but then the chill returned to her heart, recalling Tom's smile as he sat beside the new owner of the house; and the memory of her own promise to Guy came sweeping back, reminding her that her part of the bargain was still to be fulfilled.

She wandered through the deserted building, looking again at the beauty of the craftmanship of the wooden carving, the stonework, the lines of the impeccable architecture. Her appreciation blossomed in spite of her unhappiness, and she was unaware of anything except the atmosphere of the haunted rooms she explored.

Then, as before, a figure jumped from behind a door as she passed through a spacious landing, and she cried out as the present returned again, with all its unresolved problems. Manny grinned as usual, cook-a-hoop with news that came tumbling out in a rapid gunshot of words. "It's all O.K! It's been bought by a charity — won't be knocked down after all — we can all stay jest as we are! Great, eh, Miss?"

For a long moment she couldn't take in the good news, then Manny flung himself at her in a ferocious bear-hug. "Wake-up, you look all funny!" He planted a juicy kiss on her cheek and that aroused her apathy. Impossible not to share the joy in those brilliant dark eyes, that wide, monkey-grin.

"Oh, Manny — yes it *is* great news — a charity! That's marvellous; what sort of charity is it?"

"Fer the disabled, dunno any more, but Tom Hewitt, he got hold of them, see, and that's how it all happened. That fair bird in the boots liked the idea — and liked him, too, so they say — " Manny turned smartly, his ears keener than Robin's. "Wattzat?"

Footsteps sounded in the wall of the

hall below, and then started climbing the staircase. Manny rushed to the bannister rail and peered over. "Your two chaps, that's who!"

Robin's heart raced, and then relaxed as familiar voices reached her. "Are you there, Robin?" She waited for them to appear, wondering, but knowing instinctively who they must be. Guy and Derek, of course. Not Tom — what reason would Tom have for wanting to see her any more now? His problems were over. Hers were still unresolved.

She smiled stiffly and took Derek's outstretched hand, knowing from his expression that the moment of reckoning was here. "Robin, I'm sorry. I've been a so-and-so, I know I have . . . "

It was a familiar routine and she knew it by heart from past experience. But this time, it took a little longer than usual to thaw the anger and resentment she felt towards him. She kept him dangling, watching his face cloud as her immediate acceptance of his apology wasn't forthcoming. He started bragging to cover his uncertainty. "Well it's all over now; Sentry House stays as it is, so

I gather — a bit of restoration and it'll be as good as new, apparently. In a way I'm glad the deal fell through . . . for the last few days I've thought better of taking the job after all . . ."

Seeing her reluctant smile he at once asserted all the old charm, putting an arm around her, walking her down the landing, eyeing the moulded plasterwork with expert knowledge. "A pity to knock all that about eh? You were right, Robin, I've got to hand it to you. Which reminds me — want your job back? I'd be lost without you — well, take a few days, think it over, you and I are old friends, after all, I can't run a competent business without you . . . " Hastily his eyes retreated from her quizzical stare.

"Thanks, Derek." She faced him squarely, relaxing into a more friendly smile, giving no answer to his suggestion and he took the hint. "Well, I must be off — I can see I'm leaving you in good hands." He swung on his heel, looking towards Guy who stood at the end of the landing, staring out of a window, with Manny at his side pointing out aspects of the village. "Cheerio, Devenish — sorry we couldn't make a deal, but you can hardly grumble; I'd say you had come out of this sale remarkably well."

The two men shook hands and Guy's eyes flickered towards Robin. "As you say, remarkably well," he remarked quietly, with the ghost of a smile.

As Derek's feet clattered down the bare staircase, Guy muttered something to Manny and spun him a coin.

"Cor, thanks, mister — " and Manny followed Derek in leaps and bounds.

For a moment there was silence as the old house gathered its accustomed serenity about itself anew.

"Robin — "

She looked at Guy as he came towards her, a hand outstretched. Inside her, a long pent-up sigh released itself. This, then, was the end of all the fuss about Sentry House, and the beginning of the fulfillment of the bargain she had made with Guy. Unflinchingly, she went to him, her hand cold in his, her eyes meeting his honestly and bravely. She wouldn't deny him anything now. He had kept his promise, and she would keep hers.

"Guy — thank you . . . " She stumbled over the words, but he seemed to understand.

Pulling her close, he looked deep into her eyes. "You're pleased that Sentry's future is settled, of course you are." He kissed her forehead lightly, then, dropping her hands, retreated along the length of the landing, until he turned, to lean against the far window sill. His voice came from a distance, low, with the familiar vibrant tone, but somehow strangely disturbed. "Stay where you are, Robin — please, it's easier this way, better for me to keep away from you."

"But Guy, we agreed — if you gave up the idea of developing Sentry, then you and I — "

"I know."

She heard the pain in his voice and began, almost unwillingly, to understand; she stood quite still, her hands clutching at the bannister rail for support. "So why are you over there? While I'm still here? When I've just said . . . "

He interrupted her sharply. "Because if you come a step nearer I shall give way to my baser instincts!" The laugh didn't quite hide the depth of feeling in his words.

"You mean — you don't want me?"

"Of course I want you! Dear God, Robin, I shall always want you! No, stay where you are — "

She stared down the landing, thinking this must be the weirdest betrothal scene on record. Betrothal? But he wasn't acting like a lover . . .

"I've been watching you, Robin, my darling, watching you and thinking things over, and I realise it's no good hoping you would ever be happy with me. I know what Sentry House has come to mean to you, and the village, too, and today I saw something else, something I've made myself avoid facing up to ever since you and I first met." His eyes held hers and she felt quite helpless, like a puppet controlled by a master hand, unable to move of her own accord.

What was he saying? His face was suddenly sad and vulnerable and utterly unlike the Guy she thought she knew. "I watched the way you smiled at Tom Hewitt, and that was it."

The flat, resigned words seemed to

reach her from far away. So it had been that obvious — and had Tom realised it, too? Now the truth was out, Robin allowed herself the luxury of acknowledging the wonderful, but hopeless fact that she did, indeed, love Tom.

Guy came towards her, then stopped at the head of the stairs. "I guess I really do love you, Robin — for the first time in my life I can say that quite truly — and yet I don't get the girl! Quite a joke, really." His voice was tinged with humour, but Robin, so acutely aware of the feelings behind his words, understood what he was suffering.

Her eyes were misty, and she would have gone to him, but he turned quickly away, stepping down into the well of the wide, sweeping staircase.

"No, don't say anything. I've never been particularly charitable or altruistic before, and I have a feeling you could easily persuade me out of it if you tried! Just understand, though, that you're free — I'm making no demands on you. None at all. In fact, in a way, I'm glad I've managed to get through this peculiar situation so unscathed — in future I'll be far more careful before I offer my hand and my heart to a girl I've only known a few days . . . !"

His parting words were as casual and uncaring as if she meant nothing to him, nothing at all, but Robin knew otherwise. For a second he turned back as he went down the stairs, and their eyes met. She knew she would always remember this moment, and a lump came into her throat. She bent over the bannister in time to see him reach the hall below. "Guy . . . " Her voice floated in the quiet air, and he looked up again. He smiled briefly, and she waved, suddenly speechless, and that was all. The next minute she heard the front door creak, and then his footsteps, brisk and fast on the gravel drive, slowly crunching away, out of her life. And she hadn't even thanked him, or said goodbye . . .

The silence grew oppressive. She longed abruptly for sunlight and fresh air. Sentry House had played its part — now she was ready to leave its shelter. She went out, heading instinctively for the smudge of white cottage walls beneath the copse at the far end of the grounds. Perhaps Mrs Hannaman would have a friendly word, to help fill the aching void within her. Guy had gone, Sentry House was safe, and she was in love with Tom, who certainly didn't care a fig for her.

Robin laughed almost hysterically as she walked across the long stretch of parkland and wondered what she was going to do with the rest of her life. Then, abruptly, she knew; Derek had offered her her job back. The old threads were waiting to be picked up, and perhaps that was all she could ask for.

Mrs Hannaman was at the door, shading her eyes against the unlikely winter sun. "Thought it was you — I never forget a face. Come in, the kettle's on — wonderful news about the old house, so I've heard. Now things will go back to how they used to be — no more changes!"

Robin smiled numbly. Village gossip certainly spread fast. Politely she refused the invitation to have some tea. What she really needed now was solitude in which to think out her next move. She was alone, without transport; she must get a taxi, then a train from Exeter, and so home . . . funny, but it was still difficult to think of the flat in London as home.

Mrs Hannaman chatted on. "Yes, going to be a proper home again — a home for poor disabled souls, just like it was once a home for those unmarried mothers."

Inside Robin a chord vibrated, alerting her to something important. "That photo," she remembered, "the one you showed me — was that taken when Sentry was that sort of a home?"

"I think so my dear." The old face grew shrewd. "Did you know anyone here in those days, then?"

Robin relaxed, a tiny germ of new serenity growing deep within her. She would never really know, although it could have been possible. "No, Mrs Hannaman." But she knew this moment was a watershed in her life; at long last she was able to accept the fact that her mother had been unmarried and that she herself was illegitimate. And even if it was only fantasy to surmise she might have actually been born in Sentry House, at least it helped to explain the strong link she felt with the old place. She smiled at Mrs Hannaman's curious face. "Sorry, I'm day-dreaming . . . I'd better go, I've got lots of things to do. Cheerio, Mrs Hannaman — "

"Goodbye, my dear. Pop in whenever you're around, the kettle's always on."

Robin waved and turned back towards the great trees that shaded the grounds. Impossible to tell Mrs Hannaman that she would never be in Sennerton again. A voice, yelling at her, banished the quick pang of self-pity, as Manny raced up.

"I lost you!" he said thickly, mouth full of potato crisps. "Didn't you have any dinner?"

"No — can I have some of yours?" They chewed companionably as they walked back along the bank of the stream, and then Manny rushed off towards the distant summerhouse. "I'll tell Mum you're coming fer a cuppa — give her ten minutes to get the best china out, O.K., Miss?"

"O.K., Manny, I'll be there."

She lingered by the chuckling water, alone again, wondering at the spin of fortune's wheel which had brought her to Sennerton, only to have to leave it for ever after so short a time. She had wandered off into a wistful daydream when a splash in the water broke the spell. Staring down the bank, she saw a sleek, grey-brown form swimming strongly away. "The otters — they're back!" Her joy was immense and touched with something she was unable to put a name to.

So the otters, too, had come back to Sentry House for sanctuary, just as she had done. Staring down at the fast-flowing stream, she couldn't see the animal any more, but her thoughts were happy ones.

She was so engrossed that Tom's footsteps didn't arouse her. He threw his arms around her waist, and the sudden shock of discovering him behind her made her react over-violently. "Let me go, damn you!" She pulled free and whirled around, meeting a pair of icy blue eyes.

"Sorry," said Tom, not sounding the slightest bit sorry, and standing his ground.

Robin caught her breath, not sure how to handle the situation. "I didn't mean . . . " she began cautiously, and then stopped. Why bother to explain? It was over, after all. He had saved his precious Sentry House and he had that expensive blonde to unleash his passions on — so why had he come here, if not just to have the last word? A typical Tom Hewitt attitude; yes, of course, that must be it.

Coolly, she stared him out. "You frightened the otter away."

His face showed surprise and then pleasure, but the icy blue chips were still unforgiving. "I'm glad they're back — the unexpected *can* happen, you see."

She frowned. "What's that supposed to mean? It's not like you to talk in riddles."

"It's no riddle — a true statement of fact." He came a step nearer and she retreated towards a small birch tree overhanging the stream. "Look, it's budding; first tree to show green in the spring." He touched the purple-brown twigs with surprisingly gentle fingers and she glanced at the tiny swelling on the end of each branch.

Inside her a familiar pain began to ache. Damn Tom Hewitt. This wasn't the time to play games: she had made up her mind where her future lay now — back in London, picking up the threads where she had stupidly dropped them. She edged around the tree, putting the tangle of bare branches between them.

Tom stared at her through the network of twigs and she saw, with a recurrence of the pain, that he was smiling. The smile that meant he was very angry, but determined not to let it show. Suddenly she sighed, taken off-guard; how well she understood him, this obstinate, difficult man . . .

Tom's hands pounced, engulfing the birch sapling, his fingers grasping her arms, imprisoning her. He said forcefully, with a laugh in the words, "What a perverse creature you are! I waited ages for you to leave Sentry House, thinking you'd surely come out from sanctuary with your head screwed on the right way at long last! I was certain that you would come and find me — and instead *I* have to come looking for *you*: and you're being as difficult to land as a slippery fish . . . Robin, stop pulling, I have no intention of letting you go."

She glared through the twigs, unable to think properly with his hands about her. She had been so firm in her resolve to return to London — until he touched her. But now . . .

"Damn you!" She muttered bitterly, her arms sore from the hard grip of his hands.

"Damn away." He smiled in the familiar hateful, masterful way. "But I shan't let you go." Through the bending, rustling branches, his eyes sought hers and held them fast. "Not ever," he added grimly. Suddenly the ice-blue chips melted. "Don't fight any more, my lovely girl — it's such a waste of time. You'd be much better off loving me instead — and you know it . . . "

Robin opened her mouth to let out a spirited tirade, telling him exactly what she thought of him, but the words turned sour before they were uttered. Wearily she smiled, aware with great certainty and humility that he was right. Rude and arrogant he might be at times, quick-tempered and domineering, but she loved him.

"Yes, Tom, I know." Quietly she stood there surrendering herself, allowing him to pull her from behind the birch tree and into the strong, delicious warmth of his arms.

"Marry me?" he asked huskily, tipping her face up to within an inch of his own.

Commonsense struggled for a hearing in her bewildered but ecstatic mind. "Yes! I mean no! Who's the blonde who bought Sentry House? You said she was very special and I thought . . . "

He roared with laughter and closed her mouth with a long hard kiss.

Coming up for air, she tried again. "Tom, stop it! There's so much to explain — "

"Nonsense. It's all as plain as a pikestaff. The blonde, as you call her, is Annie, Sarah's godmother, and of course she's special — we were almost brought up together for one thing, and for another, anyone who's willing to spend a recently inherited fortune on a mouldy old ruin, with the idea of making it into a home for disabled kids, has to be *very* special. You'll like Annie, she's all right.

Nothing else to worry about, is there?"

Robin looked at him and thought her heart would burst with joy. She said weakly, "Well — no — I don't think so . . . "

"Then answer my question, woman. Marry me?"

She smiled. "Yes please. As soon as you like. Oh, Tom — " Pulling his face down, she kissed him thoroughly.

Manny's abashed voice sounded from behind a large beech tree, half afraid yet bursting with curiosity. "Mum's made the tea," he ventured, looking first at Robin's bemused smile and then at Tom's triumphant grin. "But if you don't want to come, well, I'll tell her — "

Tom hugged Robin to him in a final embrace then took her hand, pulling her away from the stream, over the lush grass towards the gravel drive and the Lee's summerhouse.

"Let's have a party!" he said jubilantly. "Everyone must come, Manny, go and collect your family — and bring the teapot with you — and then round up old Bert and anyone else you can find!" He threw Robin a wicked glance. "Janet will have the shock of her life! Sarah will be thrilled, and you can meet Annie."

Robin's face was dubious, but only for a second. As Manny hurtled off to spread the good news, Tom turned and kissed her again. When they finally drew apart, both instinctively glanced at the shadowy mass of Sentry House looming at the far end of the drive. They shared an understanding smile, knowing the dream would come true, after all.

"Lots of kids learning to walk properly," said Tom gently.

"Like Sarah."

"Donkeys and ponies in the stables — "

"Bert Woodall supplying the cabbages!" Robin's eyes sparkled.

" — and sanctuary offered to anyone who's interested." Tom tucked her arm in his. "Well, that's all for the future, but now — "

He pointed ahead, to where the mouse-brown thatch of Well Farm shone in the frail winter sunlight. "Come on, my lovely girl, I'm taking you home."

THE WILDERNESS WALK
Sheila Bishop

Stifling unpleasant memories of a misbegotten romance in Cleave with Lord Francis Aubrey, Lavinia goes on holiday there with her sister. The two women are thrust into a romantic intrigue involving none other than Lord Francis.

THE RELUCTANT GUEST
Rosalind Brett

Ann Calvert went to spend a month on a South African farm with Theo Borland and his sister. They both proved to be different from her first idea of them, and there was Storr Peterson — the most disturbing man she had ever met.

ONE ENCHANTED SUMMER
Anne Tedlock Brooks

A tale of mystery and romance and a girl who found both during one enchanted summer.

CLOUD OVER MALVERTON
Nancy Buckingham

Dulcie soon realises that something is seriously wrong at Malverton, and when violence strikes she is horrified to find herself under suspicion of murder.

AFTER THOUGHTS
Max Bygraves

The Cockney entertainer tells stories of his East End childhood, of his RAF days, and his post-war showbusiness successes and friendships with fellow comedians.

MOONLIGHT
AND MARCH ROSES
D. Y. Cameron

Lynn's search to trace a missing girl takes her to Spain, where she meets Clive Hendon. While untangling the situation, she untangles her emotions and decides on her own future.

NURSE ALICE IN LOVE
Theresa Charles

Accepting the post of nurse to little Fernie Sherrod, Alice Everton could not guess at the romance, suspense and danger which lay ahead at the Sherrod's isolated estate.

POIROT INVESTIGATES
Agatha Christie

Two things bind these eleven stories together — the brilliance and uncanny skill of the diminutive Belgian detective, and the stupidity of his Watson-like partner, Captain Hastings.

LET LOOSE THE TIGERS
Josephine Cox

Queenie promised to find the long-lost son of the frail, elderly murderess, Hannah Jason. But her enquiries threatened to unlock the cage where crucial secrets had long been held captive.

THE TWILIGHT MAN
Frank Gruber

Jim Rand lives alone in the California desert awaiting death. Into his hermit existence comes a teenage girl who blows both his past and his brief future wide open.

DOG IN THE DARK
Gerald Hammond

Jim Cunningham breeds and trains gun dogs, and his antagonism towards the devotees of show spaniels earns him many enemies. So when one of them is found murdered, the police are on his doorstep within hours.

THE RED KNIGHT
Geoffrey Moxon

When he finds himself a pawn on the chessboard of international espionage with his family in constant danger, Guy Trent becomes embroiled in moves and countermoves which may mean life or death for Western scientists.

TIGER TIGER
Frank Ryan

A young man involved in drugs is found murdered. This is the first event which will draw Detective Inspector Sandy Woodings into a whirlpool of murder and deceit.

CAROLINE MINUSCULE
Andrew Taylor

Caroline Minuscule, a medieval script, is the first clue to the whereabouts of a cache of diamonds. The search becomes a deadly kind of fairy story in which several murders have an other-worldly quality.

LONG CHAIN OF DEATH
Sarah Wolf

During the Second World War four American teenagers from the same town join the Army together. Forty-two years later, the son of one of the soldiers realises that someone is systematically wiping out the families of the four men.

THE LISTERDALE MYSTERY
Agatha Christie

Twelve short stories ranging from the light-hearted to the macabre, diverse mysteries ingeniously and plausibly contrived and convincingly unravelled.

TO BE LOVED
Lynne Collins

Andrew married the woman he had always loved despite the knowledge that Sarah married him for reasons of her own. So much heartache could have been avoided if only he had known how vital it was to be loved.

ACCUSED NURSE
Jane Converse

Paula found herself accused of a crime which could cost her her job, her nurse's reputation, and even the man she loved, unless the truth came to light.

BUTTERFLY MONTANE
Dorothy Cork

Parma had come to New Guinea to marry Alec Rivers, but she found him completely disinterested and that overbearing Pierce Adams getting entirely the wrong idea about her.

HONOURABLE FRIENDS
Janet Daley

Priscilla Burford is happily married when she meets Junior Environment Minister Alistair Thurston. Inevitably, sexual obsession and political necessity collide.

WANDERING MINSTRELS
Mary Delorme

Stella Wade's career as a concert pianist might have been ruined by the rudeness of a famous conductor, so it seemed to her agent and benefactor. Even Sir Nicholas fails to see the possibilities when John Tallis falls deeply in love with Stella.

MORNING IS BREAKING
Lesley Denny

The growing frenzy of war catapults Diane Clements into a clandestine marriage and separation with a German refugee.

LAST BUS TO WOODSTOCK
Colin Dexter

A girl's body is discovered huddled in the courtyard of a Woodstock pub, and Detective Chief Inspector Morse and Sergeant Lewis are hunting a rapist and a murderer.

THE STUBBORN TIDE
Anne Durham

Everyone advised Carol not to grieve so excessively over her cousin's death. She might have followed their advice if the man she loved thought that way about her, but another girl came first in his affections.